M000187453

THE EDUCATION OF A WETBACK

MARCOS ANTONIO HERNANDEZ

Copyright © 2019 by Marcos Antonio Hernandez

All rights reserved.

No part of this book may be reproduced in any form or by any electronic or mechanical means, including information storage and retrieval systems, without written permission from the author, except for the use of brief quotations in a book review.

ISBN-13: 978-1-7320035-6-9 (Paperback edition)

ISBN-13: 978-1-7320035-5-2 (Ebook edition)

CONTENTS

CHARACTER LIST

- Alejandro (husband in family who lives/works on Jose Angel's land)
- Alfonso (Toño's younger brother, after Angel)
- Angel (Toño's immediate younger brother)
- Aracely (Beto's girlfriend of the week)
- Armando (Manuel's NYC friend, grew up with both Toño and Manuel in San Ramon)
- Arminda (wife of Manuel the hotel server)
- Azucar (snow cone stand owner)
- Benito (Toño's friend in Maryland, grew up in San Ramon)
- Beto (Toño's older brother)
- Betty (Lori's mom)
- Camila (Isabel's sister)
- Carlos (mechanic in Tijuana)
- Carmen (Toño's younger sister)
- Coleman (Jewish jeweler Manuel and Toño work for in Los Angeles)
- Delfina (Beto's girlfriend)

- Dolores (Toño's maternal cousin)
- Elsa (neighbor who sells tamales)
- Esteban (Benito's friend)
- Esteban (Toño's friend in El Salvador)
- Father Cristobal (town priest)
- Felicita (Toño's mother)
- Hector (Armando's friend)
- Hortensia Lopez (Toño's girlfriend in El Salvador)
- Gustavo (Cuban, works with Tomás to smuggle people into America)
- Isabel (Benito's fiancée/wife)
- Jorge (Manuel's brother)
- Jose Angel (Toño's father)
- Juan Antonio Hernandez, Toño
- Lillian (Toño's youngest sister/youngest sibling overall)
- Lori (Angel's manager at McDonald's; Toño's fiancee)
- Lucia (girl from town, sister of Sebastian)
- Lulu (captain of Toño's soccer team)
- Manuel (Toño's best friend and former neighbor who moved to Los Angeles)
- Manuel (a server at the hotel where Toño works)
- Maria (Toño's younger sister)
- Napoleon (takes over as Angel's roommate when Toño moves back to El Salvador)
- Paula (Hector's sister)
- Philip (manager of hotel on Frederick Road)
- Rivaldo (striker on Toño's soccer team)
- Rosa (Toño's younger sister)
- Sandra (wife in family living/working on Jose Angel's land)

- Sebastian (boy from town, brother of Lucia)
- Tio Abel (Toño's uncle)
- Tomas (Dolores's husband; smuggles people into America)
- William (manager of hotel Toño works for)

PART 1

OUT OF THE FRYING PAN

CHAPTER ONE

SOME PEOPLE ARE BORN into families lucky enough to know where their next meal will come from. They come into a world where it's possible to drive to a grocery store, park their cars, and buy whatever food they need.

Those born in less fortunate circumstances view the miracle of children through a different lens. The arrival of a child means, at first, more food is required, but along with the increased strain from the extra mouth comes the hope that there will be more hands to help provide in the future, as long as the child is a boy.

Juan Antonio Hernandez, Toño for short, was born into a world where his family has to farm for the food on their table. He wakes up in the dead of night to the buzz of insects in the trees around him, feeling like he could have found a dream if he had stayed asleep a moment longer. The nights in El Salvador are warm enough that he can sleep beneath the leaves of the banana trees even though he has the option to share a bed with his brother. He sits up and turns to the side, places his feet on the packed dirt riddled with roots, and takes three large breaths before he stands up and stretches his back.

Toño passes by his house's open patio on his way to the stone outhouse. The leaves above block the moon from lighting the way but the dirt paths around the house are so well worn from the passage of the ten members of his family that Toño's feet can follow the path without help from his eyes. The snores of his older brother reverberate through the house from the children's bedroom, reminding Toño why he sleeps alone in the hammock whenever possible.

Toño shuffles into the stand-alone structure, his eyes half open and still adjusting to the darkness.

"Wait!" Jose Angel calls out from the far corner of the space.

"Sorry," Toño says, backing out. He leans against the wall of the building and rests his head against the stone. His father has, yet again, woken up before him. On most mornings, the old man has fed the animals and is already out in the fields looking for squatters by now, but today he must have given himself extra rest.

Jose Angel exits the outhouse, struggling to buckle his pants with metal hands the size of plates, a byproduct of working the farm his entire life. He stops in the door and concentrates on the task while telling Toño, "When you're done in there go wake Beto up. You two have lots to do."

Toño wants to remark on how there's always lots to do, that this morning is like all the others, but decides it's too early to utter so many words. "Of course," he says while he waits for his father to vacate the entrance.

After Jose Angel succeeds in buckling his pants, he walks away to feed and water the family's animals: eleven cattle, twenty-one chickens, and a horse. Seven cows and eleven chickens belong to Jose Angel, the horse is owned by both Beto and Toño, and the remaining animals belong to Toño alone.

Toño's animal collection began with one chicken when he

was young. By saving, selling, and caring for them he has been able to grow his group with the support of his father. Beto doesn't have the same mind-set, and it was only after Toño convinced Beto how easy life would be with a horse that he was able to convince his brother to split the cost of one with him.

When Toño is finished in the outhouse, he gets dressed and walks towards Beto's room. His brother's snores sound as if the walls of the bedroom were built around a diesel truck. The truck eats enough food to travel from one side of El Salvador to the other but somehow manages to stay rail-thin. "Must be because my brain needs so much fuel," Beto would say whenever someone would remark on the amount of food he consumes. If Toño's parents, Jose Angel and Felicita, knew how much food their first child would require, it's doubtful they would've had their second, Toño, let alone the other seven. Then again, maybe it's because they saw how much Beto ate that they realized they would need more hands to help produce all the food.

The snores end the moment Toño places his hand on his older brother's shoulder. "It's already time? I just went to sleep!" Beto says, his voice full of energy. His stomach growls in the night, as loud as or louder than any of his snores, and Toño is certain the rest of the family has been woken up. His two younger brothers in the other bed don't even rearrange themselves in their sleep.

Beto taps his stomach twice. "Must be time to get up since I'm already hungry again," he mutters to himself. Without bothering to put any clothes on he walks in his underwear to the kitchen and eats a half dozen bananas. "Back to my old self again," he says with a grin once he's done.

Beto throws on his farm clothes and the two brothers walk into the night. Plants extend probing leaves into their path and Toño lets each one brush his leg, but Beto believes it's his duty to preserve the purity of the path by hacking away with his machete at the intruders.

"I dreamt about her again," Beto says to Toño's back as he swings his blade.

Toño doesn't respond. His brother has been dreaming about the same woman for weeks now and believes he will be able to find her in San Salvador.

"She's out there, I know it."

"Then go find her," Toño says. He wonders if, were he able to dream, he would dream about the same woman every night, the same way his brother does?

"I will. And when I move to the city to live with her you can take the farm."

This is the first time Beto has mentioned his intention to leave. The farm is the eldest brother's inheritance, or at least that's the assumption of the family.

Toño flexes his hand. "What if I don't want it? My fingers are already getting stiff. If I take the farm my hands will turn to metal too and I'm not sure I want to deal with the headache," Toño says without turning around.

"Well then, you can pass it on to Angel. And if he doesn't want it he can pass it on to Alfonso."

Toño and his brother continue on their walk around the farm in silence. The sugarcane is untouched by thieves and its leaves sway gently in the morning breeze. The sun creeps over the horizon while the brothers inspect the banana trees in the grove and find there has been no change from the day before. Between the squatters and the crop thieves the family has plenty of work just to make sure the plants reach maturity and can be sold in the market.

When the two brothers get to the plot of land given to Toño to grow crops of his own, Beto waters a nearby tree with the liquid he's been carrying in his stomach. Here, Toño grows loroco with the hope of selling it to the women who make pupusas and stuff them with the plant. His biggest fear, and the reason he checks the vines each and every day, is giant zompopo ants. Each one is the size of a fist and capable of eating a vine by itself. A swarm could be devastating. He finds the exoskeleton of one ant and crushes it under the sole of his boot with a satisfying crunch. He hopes the mangled corpse will provide enough of a deterrent to other ants who stumble upon his plot of land.

On their walk back to the house, Toño tells Beto he doesn't want the farm. "I don't want my future dependent on whether or not you stay in the capital," he says.

"What's that supposed to mean?"

"It's just that if you decide to come back, the farm would still go to you. I'm not planning my life around one of your dreams."

"And what are you going to do instead?"

"Not sure yet. I know I need to make money."

"I'm going to make my money in the capital, there's nowhere better," Beto says with confidence.

Toño nods. There is one place he can think of where he could make more money than in the capital: America.

CHAPTER TWO

"We have to go to the market," Jose Angel says when the two brothers get back.

Beto pats Toño on the back, goes into the bedroom, and emerges with a towel. Time for his morning shower. Whenever there is more work to do, extra work, Toño is the one who is responsible for the task.

"What do we need in the market?" Toño asks. His high school graduation is today, and he wants to shower before the ceremony, but he knows work comes first. Since Jose Angel pays for Toño's education the old man never thinks twice about making his son late, and Toño, not wanting to attract attention to himself, never told his family about the importance of the day.

"I used the last of the pesticide on some zompopo ants I saw. We need to get more."

The can that holds the pesticide has permanent dents from where Jose Angel's fingers have dug into the side.

"Let's go then," Toño says to his father.

"Grab the big one," Jose Angel instructs Toño with a nod to the large plastic drum, a forearm's length in diameter and an arm's length deep. Two ropes are drilled into the sides of the container to make it easier to carry, but once full, easier doesn't mean easy.

The market is an hour's walk away. Father and son don't talk to each other on the walk, but Jose Angel greets each and every person they pass. Everyone in the town knows the old man because his house is one of the few dozen in the town proper, which gives the family an elevated status compared to the people who live on the outskirts or in little "villages," collections of families who decide to live close to each other in houses constructed of whatever material they can salvage. The family's status is further elevated because their house is in the exact center of the town, a fact leveraged more by Toño's mother, Felicita, than anyone else.

The market is busy for a Tuesday. Toño and his father walk to the pesticide seller and ask how much to fill up both the can and the drum. While Jose Angel and the salesman haggle over price, Toño looks at boots for sale arranged on a rug right next him.

"Interested in a new pair?" the man says, looking at Toño's feet. He is sitting cross-legged on the far corner of the rug. Rudimentary crutches lean against the stone wall behind him and Toño wonders which of the man's legs doesn't work.

Toño leans back to inspect his own worn-out pair of boots. Mud and excrement are caked around the soles, and the leather uppers have both dark stains from only God knows where and chemical stains from where pesticide has dripped onto his feet. He can't afford a new pair himself, and he knows his father won't approve of the expense.

"What size are you?" the man says. His words pull Toño away from the inspection of his feet.

Toño and the man meet eyes. "Not sure," he says.

"Why are you so sad?" the salesman asks.

"What do you mean?" Toño says.

9

"Your eyes. They look like a sad dog."

Toño glares at the man. "I'm thinking, that's all. Haven't you ever seen a man think?"

"I've seen men think before and this isn't it."

"What do you know?" Toño says. He turns back to his father in time to see the exchange of money and watches the salesman fill both containers with liquid while trying to keep the sadness in his eyes from seeping into the containers of pesticide.

Jose Angel grabs the can, his metal fingers aligning with the indents already present, and tells Toño to take the drum.

Toño grabs both pieces of rope, stands up, leans back, and hears the liquid slosh inside. He follows his father back home along the same route they used to get there, each small step causing the liquid to move in the open drum. Toño watches the liquid, careful not to spill a drop. At first he counts his steps by counting to ten over and over again, but once he counts to ten ten times he loses track and treats each ten as a new, independent set of steps.

"I have to set it down," Toño says to his father when their town is in sight.

"Set it down? For what?"

"The rope is digging into my hands," Toño says, shaking his hands out. Deep creases run through the middle of his palms from where the rope has dug into his skin.

Jose Angel sets the can down, grabs the two pieces of rope, and lifts the drum with ease. "I don't feel a thing," he says.

"Of course you don't, your hands are already metal. Mine haven't been hardened yet."

"I didn't raise you to be soft."

"I just need a minute."

Jose Angel grabs Toño by the throat and lifts his son's chin, the metal cold against Toño's skin. He stares into his son's eyes and in slow words tells Toño to pick up the drum.

Toño drops his gaze and his father releases him. He stares into the pesticide as the two men continue their walk back home and is horrified when a single tear drops from his face into the liquid. His hands have lost all feeling by the time they get back to the house in the middle of the town.

Jose Angel doesn't stay in the house for more than a moment. He takes the can of pesticide and goes back to where he used the last of it on the ants, searching for more that could still be in the area.

There is a circle where the drum sits in the corner of the patio, and Toño is careful to put the container back in the exact right place where it was. He wonders if the tear that fell into the liquid has contaminated the entire batch. He dips a small metal cup into the liquid and walks around looking for a test subject. He finds a small centipede and splashes it with the contents of the cup. Most insects, when sprayed with the pesticide, scurry away before they die. The centipede in Toño's experiment doesn't even move. Even though the centipede's belly drags on the ground when it walks, it somehow manages to get even lower to the ground after being splashed by Toño.

It takes three days for the centipede to starve to death, alive the whole time but too sad to move.

CHAPTER THREE

EVEN THOUGH IT'S only Tuesday, Toño pulls out his Sunday outfit for his last trip to school—his good pair of jeans and a white button-down with vertical blue stripes. There isn't enough time for him to shower, he's late as it is, so he takes off his work shirt and wipes his armpits with it, steals a spray of cologne from his father, and changes into his chosen outfit. The boots he wears are the same boots he had on before, the only pair he owns.

Toño says goodbye to his mother and younger siblings the same way he has every school day for years and begins the hour-long march along the main road. Dust from the road kicks up every time a bus passes, dust that was present hours before on his trip to the market but is now noticed because of the pressure to look presentable. By the time Toño arrives at the school, he is covered with a thin layer of the road.

The entire school is seated in the courtyard. The teachers sit in a single row of chairs split down the middle by a podium and face rows of chairs for the students and their families. The last time the courtyard was arranged in this manner was for the funeral of a politician who had fought with the priest of the only church in town. After the man refused a deathbed apology, the church issued a statement saying the funeral couldn't be held within its walls. Toño notes how the atmosphere of today's ceremony has the same feeling as the politician's funeral, with less black.

Toño walks past the mass of people, goes into the four-room building, and heads straight for the bathroom. He wets his hair and runs a comb missing two teeth over his scalp. He flushes his face with water and brown sediment collects on the bottom of the porcelain sink.

As Toño walks outside, the headmaster calls for everyone's attention to the front in the same tone of voice as the priest calls for the attention of his flock on Sunday. There is an empty chair in front and Toño hurries to take a seat. His name is called out from the back of the courtyard and there, standing up, is the entire rest of his family. Who told them?

The ceremony lasts two hours but feels like two days. Between the heat, Toño's early morning, and the voices of speaker after speaker, Toño has trouble keeping his eyes open. Twice he gets an elbow to the ribs when his head leans forward and his chin touches his chest. When his name is called, he walks to the podium to receive his diploma and hears the shouts of his younger siblings from the back. He flashes them a smile.

When the ceremony ends, Toño goes to see his family. "How did you know?" he asks his mother.

"How could we not know? Everyone except you has been talking about it for weeks!" Toño's younger sister Carmen says.

"I didn't want to bother everyone with coming. It's really not a big deal."

"Not a big deal!" Jose Angel says, annoyed. "Of course it's a big deal. Don't you remember what we did for Beto's graduation? There was a party and everything."

"I do remember, and I didn't want all of that," Toño says. He says a quick prayer to himself, hopeful there isn't a party planned.

"You and Beto are different. We were thinking about having dinner with the family, that's all. Unless you want a party."

"I don't."

"Ok then, it's settled. No party. Dinner tonight," Jose Angel says.

Toño has plans to see Hortensia, a young girl from outside of town, but doesn't mention them. As long as he is back in time for the meal, nobody will wonder where he went.

Toño and his family wait while Beto and Jose Angel talk to members of the town who come over to say hello. Once they are finished, the family walks back home together.

"So what are you going to do now?" Toño's brother Angel asks.

"What do you mean?"

"Well, you're done with school."

"Not sure," Toño says. "I was playing around with the idea of going to the university in San Salvador and becoming an agronomist, but we can't afford it."

Jose Angel stays silent.

"Guess you'll do the same thing you do every day: work the farm," Beto says with a satisfied smirk.

"Always plenty of work to do," Jose Angel says.

Toño realizes he just sat through what could have been his own funeral—except he doesn't want to go into politics and can still go to church.

A bus honks from behind the family and they move to one side of the road to let the vehicle pass. The Hernandez clan continue their trip through a cloud of dust left behind by the bus.

"I was thinking about going to America," Toño says into the

silence around the family. His eyes stare at the road ahead, not quite on the ground and not quite on the horizon.

"Were you now?" Beto says.

Toño's mother can't hide her disbelief. Tears well in her eyes and fall to the dusty road every time her right foot strikes the earth.

Toño's younger brothers and sisters begin to pepper Toño with questions. Rosa coughs and adds more dust to the cloud ahead of them.

"When will you leave?"

"What will you do?"

"Where will you live?"

"Are you going to learn English?"

Toño puts his hands in the air. "I'm not sure of anything yet, it's just an idea. All I know is that I need to make money. There's no better place to do it than in America."

The muscles in Jose Angel's jaw contract and relax, and Toño wonders which words his father fights to hold inside.

Beto laughs and pats Toño on the back. "You always have a trick up your sleeve, brother."

CHAPTER FOUR

THE FAMILY DISPERSES as soon as they get into town. The younger siblings all go off to play with their friends without changing out of their church clothes, with directions from Felicita to all be home in time for dinner. Beto, Toño, and the parents go into their house, with the youngest sibling, Lillian, following Felicita like a shadow. Both Beto and Jose Angel change their clothes and head out: Beto to meet up with his girlfriend; Jose Angel to check on his plants.

Before Toño can go into his room to change for his afternoon with Hortensia, Felicita tells him to sit down.

"What do you want for dinner?" she asks.

"You know I don't care. Whatever you want to make."

"Come on, I know you have favorites. What comes to mind?"

Toño stares out the back patio of their house, to the stone oven and his hammock in the distance. "Maybe soup?"

"I can do soup," Felicita replies. "Any particular kind?"

"De mondongo?"

"Hmm . . . I'll have to talk to the neighbor to see if they have any for me to buy, but I should be able to." The cabinet that holds the pots and pans overhears their conversation and opens on its own as Felicita approaches. She bends down and takes out a pot deep enough for Lillian to stand up inside. "Anything to go along with the soup?"

"Tortillas."

"Tortillas!" Lillian exclaims.

"We have tortillas with every meal, you know that," Felicita says.

"Then whatever else you want to make," Toño says. "I have to get ready."

Toño considers changing into another outfit in order to save the outfit to be used again on Sunday but decides the clothes he has on will already need to be washed so he might as well keep them on. He unbuttons one more button, exposing the few chest hairs he has been able to grow.

The sun is on its way down when Toño sets out to meet Hortensia Lopez at the soccer field. They have been seeing each other in secret for over a year. They follow a rigid schedule, imposed by Toño, and tonight is one of the nights they dedicate to seeing each other. Neither of them would call the days they see each other sacred, but neither of them would break the scheduled date either.

Hortensia lives in one of the barrios outside of town. The soccer field is closer to her house than to Toño's, but he doesn't want to be in the town when they see each other because he never knows where his brothers and sisters could be playing. She is shorter than Toño and skinny from years of never knowing where her next meal will come from. There are rumors she has made a deal with the devil, because her lips and nails are bright red, not because they are painted, which she could never afford, but because of a natural color that showed up after puberty.

"Toño!" Hortensia cries out when they see each other. They

exchange a quick hug while Toño looks around to see if anyone is watching.

The pair part and Toño looks past her. "Your eyes are always searching," she says. "Like a hungry dog looking for his next meal . . ."

"I'm always hungry," Toño jokes.

"Or looking to see if he will get in trouble for breaking the rules," Hortensia says with sadness. She frowns, her red bottom lip jutting out farther than Toño thought possible.

This isn't the first time Toño has heard her talk this way, and he chooses to ignore instead of engage. Satisfied they are alone, he takes her hand and leads her on a walk away from the town along a road on the edge of a field of sugarcane. The pair take a left turn onto a dirt path, their usual route, headed towards the backside of his family's land.

"How was your graduation today?" Hortensia asks.

"It was good. My family showed up."

"They did? That was nice of them," Hortensia says, her voice trailing off. She stopped going to school after the eighth grade so she could stay at home and take care of the house with her mother with plans to one day marry and become the caretaker of her own home.

"What are you going to do now that you're done?" Hortensia asks.

"Not sure. Beto wants me to take over the farm but I'm not sure. I was thinking about going to America. Manuel went up last month and I could stay with him." Manuel and Toño had been neighbors and friends for years until Manuel left last year to live in San Salvador. Two months ago his friend moved again, this time to Los Angeles, a lifelong dream. Toño remembers how Manuel used every opportunity to practice his English when he lived in the town, and now he gets to practice every day.

Hortensia's sadness sends a ripple through the field of sugarcane around her. She reaches out to touch the vibrating leaves with her red-tipped fingers. "So I guess we wouldn't see each other anymore."

Toño gets annoyed at her probing question and releases her hand. "Don't see how we would, I'd be in a whole other country."

"I'd miss you."

Toño doesn't respond. The silence weighs down on Hortensia's shoulders, causing a slight hunch in her back as they walk.

"The carnival is supposed to be here this weekend," she says. "Will you take me?"

"I can't. We have a soccer game against the police officers in San Salvador and I'll have to spend money on travel. Nothing left over for carnivals."

Hortensia hooks her left arm under Toño's right and lays her head on his shoulder. "It's too public, I know."

"We aren't talking about this right now."

"When will we? We've been sneaking around for over a year. Do you even talk about me with anyone else?"

"Why does it matter if I talk about you?"

"It'd be nice if you did. Not even to your closest friends?"

"Manuel knows," Toño lies.

"Manuel doesn't live here anymore. Does anyone in the town know?"

"I don't talk about you with anyone here, it's none of their business."

Hortensia waits until the lump in her throat goes away before she tells Toño she wishes their relationship wasn't a secret.

On a normal walk with Hortensia, one where she isn't questioning their future, Toño and Hortensia would stay together until the sun was almost gone beyond the horizon. Their walk would conclude back at the soccer field, where they would say goodbye and make plans for their next meeting. Today, Toño asks Hortensia if she knows the way back on her own.

"I have to be back for dinner so I'm going to walk through our land to the house. Will you be all right?"

Hortensia pulls away from Toño and stares at him. "I'll be all right," she says. "Don't worry about me."

"I won't."

Toño walks home to a waiting meal wondering if there will be enough beans for Hortensia and her family to escape going to bed hungry.

CHAPTER FIVE

Toño GETS BACK to his house while his mother is still cooking dinner. Flames lick the side of the pot of soup, and the wooden spoon inside spins on its own at the speed that Felicita taught the utensil is necessary for this dish. While the soup cooks, she makes two large piles of tortillas, one for Beto and one for the rest of the family.

Lillian plays with a child-sized broom Jose Angel has made for her, trying her best to teach the tool to move side to side with both hands on the handle without moving her arms. Felicita takes a moment to pull away from her tortilla production to show her daughter how it's done one more time.

"Watch," she says. She takes her full-sized broom in one hand and holds her arm out straight. The broom begins to tick like a metronome, back and forth, and she walks around the room as its guide. She places another hand on the handle of the broom and it begins to sweep in one direction.

"Train your broom to go back and forth with one hand first, then you can put two hands on it to tell it to sweep in one direction." She sets her broom down in the corner and goes back to her tortillas, leaving her daughter to practice. "Dinner should be ready in an hour," she says.

"Smells good," says Toño.

Lillian holds the broom with one hand and manages to convince the broom to sway from left to right. There isn't enough power behind the movement to do more than kick up some dust, but her eyes still open wide when she succeeds in teaching the broom to move at all. "Did you see that, Toño?" she says.

"I did. You are doing a great job teaching it how to act."

"Can you do it?" Lillian asks.

"He's the only one of my sons who bothered to learn," says Felicita. "Show Lillian what you can do."

Toño grabs the full-sized broom from the corner and holds it out with one hand. Its bristles bend from the downward force into the ground and powerful strokes send a rush of air through the room, causing strands of Lillian's hair to blow into her face. Toño walks around the kitchen table and only stops when Felicita yells at him for getting dust in her dough.

"You need to learn to be more delicate," she says. "The point isn't to throw dust into the air, it's to move the dust outside!"

Lillian holds her broom out with one arm and forces the bristles into the ground.

"Don't apply so much pressure," Felicita says.

Toño pulls the handle of Lillian's broom up and the bristles relax. "I don't make so much wind on purpose, I just never bothered to learn how to control the pressure."

"Do the spoons listen to you too?"

"No, they don't. I never cook so they never got the chance to know me."

"Why does the broom know you?" Lillian says.

"Before I could go out into the fields I still wanted to help.

Sweeping every morning and night was my job until I was old enough to help Dad."

Lillian nods, holds her broom at arm's length, and adopts a look of concentration.

"You weren't gone very long. I was expecting you to be back much later," Felicita says.

"I didn't want to miss dinner."

"You know we don't have dinner until the sun has gone down. You could have spent more time with her."

"With her?"

"Don't pretend like I don't know where you spend your afternoons. When Manuel moved away you stopped going anywhere in the afternoons until you started spending time with this girl from the barrio."

Toño is speechless. He thought his walks with Hortensia were a secret—he had been so careful!—but in a small town he should have known word would get out.

"What's her name?"

Toño is certain Felicita knows this information as well but decides to tell her anyways. "Hortensia Lopez."

"Hortensia," Felicita says, weighing the word on her tongue. "Does she make you happy?"

"Most of the time. She annoyed me today though, that's why I came back early."

"If she makes you happy, why do you try and keep her a secret?" Felicita says. She sets the last tortilla on the pan, walks over to the soup, and withdraws a spoonful. She blows on the liquid before tasting it. "Needs more salt," she says.

"I keep her a secret because I'm not sure if I want her in my future."

"You keep worrying about the future, Toño. All you have is the present. If she makes you happy you should be with her!"

Toño looks down at his hands and cleans dirt from under his thumbnail.

"It's because she's from the barrio, isn't it?"

"The people in the town says she's made a deal with the devil because of her red lips and nails. She can't help it though, it's natural."

"Oh, you have been spending your time with her? She only goes to church once a month, if that."

"She doesn't have nice clothes and only goes so God doesn't forget her."

"Have you told her that God doesn't care about such silly things like clothes?"

"It's not God that she worries about, it's the people in the town."

Felicita nods. "You know people looked down on your father for marrying me."

Toño has heard the story before but it's never been brought up as a direct comparison to his situation.

"I lived outside of another town, about an hour away. My family had nothing and your father . . . well, your father had this house, smack-dab in the middle of town. If your father had paid any attention to what people said about him you would never have been born!"

Toño lifts his gaze and looks at his mother. She turns her back to him and pulls the tortillas from the pan.

"So you're telling me to give her a chance? To stop keeping it a secret?"

"Only you know that. What I'm telling you is to keep an open mind. If she makes you happy then why not keep her around? People will run out of things to say, and even if they don't, who cares?"

Toño doesn't get the chance to digest her advice because she asks him to help her lift the pot of soup off the fire. He keeps the pot at arm's length so he doesn't burn himself and sets it on the stone counter.

"When your father gets back we'll eat," she says.

On cue, Jose Angel walks through the front door. "I'm starving," he says. "Where is everyone?" His nose leads him to the pot on the counter, and with metal fingers he lifts the lid to inspect its contents. His fingers are so stiff they continue to grasp the lid even after it has been placed back over the pot, and he must use his other hand to hold down the lid while he pries his fingers away. With both hands he grabs his personal wooden bowl from the shelf next to the spices. His personal wooden spoon with its extra-long handle sits inside, cleaned after the previous meal.

The rest of the children file in through the front door over the next ten minutes as if they know their father is hungry. Alfonso and Angel are covered with dirt—Felicita tells them to wash their hands, at the very least—and Beto has a smile plastered on his face. Rosa, Carmen, and Maria all have flowers in their hair and giggle about seeing one male dog hump another.

Toño eats more at dinner than he ever has before. On a normal night he tries to save some food for the younger siblings, or for the next day, but tonight Felicita has to relight the fire and cook more tortillas to keep up with his massive appetite. It's close, but he still isn't able to put down as much food as Beto.

The events of the day overtake him while he chews his last bite. He leaves his dishes on the table, not a drop of food on them, and is able to make it to his hammock before he collapses. Sleep overtakes him the moment he lies down. At some point in the night he begins to hover an inch above his bed, the weight of his secret relationship with Hortensia lifted from his soul.

CHAPTER SIX

CARNIVAL FEVER TAKES over the town for the next two days. The caravan of trucks carrying the equipment arrives early Thursday morning and parks in the center of the soccer field, ready to extend its tendrils out in every direction and transform the field into an oasis. Toño wants to experience the festivities, but he knows Hortensia will be upset if she finds out he was there without her, so he resigns himself to the fact he should stay away.

While the rest of the town talks about the carnival, the rest of Toño's soccer team, the Deers, all talk about their upcoming game. Lulu, who cofounded the team with Tono and now serves as their captain, has been able to get a bus for the two-hour trip to the capital. Toño wants to be able to enjoy the trip without having to come back to a list of tasks to do, so he spends Thursday and Friday doing all that he can in order to get ahead, the whole time preoccupied by thoughts of the best way to stop a police officer from scoring a goal. Saturday morning finds Toño, his work done, lined up with the rest of his team outside the school while they wait for the bus to arrive. Lulu is the last to show and carries with him bad news.

"The bus broke down on the way here," he informs the team.

A collective groan emanates from the group.

"And it's too late to find another way to the city. I will have to let them know we can't make it, there's no other choice."

"Not only do we miss a trip into the city, now we have to forfeit a game!" Rivaldo, the team's best striker, cries out.

"We're doing so well this season too," Toño says.

"I know, I know," says Lulu. "Now we have to win the rest of our games. If we even lose one we won't make the playoffs."

The team walks away, their heads down, in every direction away from the school. Toño's walk back home will take him the next hour. He could choose to take the bus now that he isn't spending any money on the trip to the capital, but he decides to save the expense and walk.

Toño thinks about Hortensia while he walks. Now that he doesn't have to go to his game, should he see if she wants to go to the carnival with him? Everyone will be there tonight, and he can't decide whether or not he wants the rest of the town to find out about their relationship in such a public fashion.

Has she already made plans to go without him? She probably has. He should just go by himself. Maybe Beto wants to go with him, or one of his other siblings. Should he feel guilty if he decides to go without her? It's not his fault the bus broke down and gave him a free afternoon.

The house is empty when Toño gets back. He puts his soccer equipment back where it belongs, underneath the bed where Beto sleeps, and eats a banana before he lies in his hammock to take a quick nap.

Rosa shakes him awake in the afternoon, asking what he's doing home. "I thought you had a game today," she says, turning to walk back into the kitchen.

Toño sits up. "I did, but the bus broke down so I came home. Where is everyone?"

Rosa stops walking but doesn't turn around. "Mom went to church, Dad is in the field, Beto went to the carnival . . . and I don't know where everyone else is. Dad said we are going to the carnival tonight, are you going to come too?"

"I might. I was thinking about going now."

"With Beto?"

"If he's there. If not I'll just walk around. Want to come?"

"I'm going to wait to go with Dad. He said he would buy me a pastry," Rosa says as she walks back into the house.

Toño walks to the carnival, the whole time trying to convince himself he has no reason to feel guilty. Each step towards the carnival is more difficult than the last. He stops before walking onto the transformed soccer field, his feet sunken into the dirt road up to his ankles. When he turns he sees a line of footsteps behind him getting progressively shallower the closer to his house they are. This is common during the rainy season, when the road turns to mud, but in the dry heat of summer he can't imagine how heavy he must be to sink down the way he is. Not even the carnival's truck made tracks on the hard dirt, but his footsteps are heavy enough to pierce the earth's crust.

The dusty field is dotted with booths, stages, and rides. It isn't quite sundown and there are already men passed out on the ground, drunk. There are so many people walking between the attractions that they must have come from neighboring towns. Toño remembers Hortensia's previous boyfriend is from the next town over. As much as Toño likes to think he could walk away from Hortensia, the thought of her in another man's arms makes his blood boil.

Dread at running into Hortensia, and the disappointment it would cause her, makes Toño's eyes extend halfway from their sockets and his ears grow twice their normal size on high alert for her shadow. As he inspects the sea of eyes, on the lookout for hers, a familiar hand pats him on the back.

"Toño!" Beto says.

"Hey," Toño says, distracted by his search.

"I wondered if you would show up. I heard the bus broke down," Beto continues.

Beto's girlfriend this week, Aracely, stands on the other side of Beto. She catches Toño's eyes and nods. "We were just about to get some food. Want to join us?" she says.

They buy small honey pastries and two sausages from a local woman, Toño eating his own and Beto sharing his with Aracely. Toño wonders why Beto bothers to share his food but doesn't bring it up. They end up near the rides. Out of nowhere, Beto grabs Toño's shoulder and pulls him back behind the booth of a local psychic.

"What the hell is wrong with you?" Toño says.

Aracely realizes she is alone in the path between booths and looks around before she finds the two brothers and walks towards them without saying a word.

"Shh. Look," Beto says. He points to the Ferris wheel up ahead.

"I don't see anything special," Toño says, annoyed.

"Wait for it . . . there!"

Toño looks at the bottom car of the wheel. Hortensia is alongside her previous boyfriend, red lips surrounding white teeth as she laughs.

Blood rockets up to Toño's face. The pressure builds while Toño struggles to control himself. A valve inside breaks and blood begins to trickle from his left eye, which he wipes away with a hand still greasy from the sausage.

"How do you know about her?"

"Everyone knows."

"You think I care?" Toño lies.

"That's your woman! She's only here with him because she thinks you are in San Salvador. Aren't you going to say something to her?"

"No. She can do what she wants." What good would words do? He had heard the rumors but chose to ignore them. She took his virginity but he didn't take hers, he knew that, but no God-fearing woman would have red lips and nails the way she does. He thought she was different.

"I've told you this before: women will take what they can get, brother."

Aracely pretends not to hear Beto's advice.

Toño stares as the two of them go around the Ferris wheel two more times. "I'm going home," he says.

"Don't be like that, Toño," Aracely says. "My friend will be here later, I can introduce you to her. She's very nice!"

"Forget about her!" Beto urges. "Let's just have fun."

"My stomach hurts," Toño says. Stomach or heart, all he knows is it's something inside.

Toño leaves the carnival in a daze. On the walk back home he has to stop to throw up into the ditch on the side of the road. Once the sausage then the pastry comes back up, Toño tries to stand upright and continue on his way, but as soon as he's vertical he has to double over again. After a few dry heaves, rose petals spew from his mouth and cover his half-digested food. The delicate petals remain unchanged until they are washed away a week and one day later.

CHAPTER SEVEN

THOUGHTS of the future plague Toño's mind while he walks through his family's land Thursday morning. His father found a piece of trash near the coconut trees the day before and wants Toño to check to see if there are new signs of thieves in the grove.

"Double check, I hope it isn't those kids from the barrio again," Jose Angel said to Toño before leaving for the market.

The coconuts are untouched and there are no signs of human activity in the area. Toño continues through the oranges, bananas, and sugarcane, looking for anything out of the ordinary, but everything is as it should be. No signs of animals or insects, let alone humans.

Toño knows he has to leave the town and decides he has two options. One, he could talk to his father about going to the university again; or two, he could go to the United States and make money. He believes his father can't afford to pay for more school since he has so many kids still left to go through high school, but since his father never shares the details of his financial situation he can't be sure.

He wishes he could talk to Beto about the situation. If his brother had it his way, Toño would take over the farm. Each of his days, for the rest of his days, would be the same. Wake up, work the farm, wake up, work the farm, over and over again until the day he dies.

"If I stay, how long would it take to get a farm of my own?" he asks the vegetation around him as he hacks at the undergrowth with his machete. Swinging his blade interrupts his train of thought and brings him back to the words Beto said. Who is he to decide Toño's future?

An iguana is sunbathing alone on a rock in a rare spot of sunlight under the trees. Toño approaches the lizard and it doesn't move. Toño pokes the lizard with his machete and it pretends to scurry away. The lizard doesn't live on the rock; he shows up long enough to gather warmth then goes about his business.

Toño informs his family of his decision at dinner that night. "I'm going to the United States," he says. Time stops in the room for everyone but him. He savors a bite of tortilla, knowing in the near future he will be far away from his mother's cooking.

Toño has eaten three tortillas by the time the hands on the clock begin to move again. Felicita stares at him with her mouth open wide, exposing food in various stages of being chewed.

Jose Angel stands up and grabs a warm bottle of beer, a rarity since years before when he stopped drinking one with dinner every night. He sits back down, cracks it open, and takes a long drink.

Beto laughs. "How are you going to do that?" he asks.

"I'll talk to Tomas. He'll take me." Tomas, husband of Dolores, Toño's cousin on his mother's side. It's no secret what the alcoholic man does for money: he takes immigrants across the border.

"So you've thought about this?" Jose Angel says, the first noise he's made since opening his beer.

"I have, and I've decided. I will stay there for five years then come back and use the money I make to buy a farm." Then, he thinks, I will have something no woman would risk losing by running around behind my back.

"Does this have anything to do with the Ferris wheel yesterday?" Beto says.

Felicita can read her second son's thoughts. She speaks, her voice no louder than a whisper. "You stopped seeing Hortensia."

"The devil-girl," says Maria.

"She's cursed," says Carmen.

"Enough, you two," Jose Angel says.

Toño sits up in his chair. "Yes, I did. She isn't worth my time."

Lillian takes a bite of her beans and rice. Then, in order from youngest to oldest, each person begins to eat again. Excluding Toño, who never stopped eating in the first place.

"When are you leaving?" Jose Angel asks.

"As soon as I sell my animals and the plants I have. It should be enough money to get me there."

Jose Angel looks to the ceiling while he calculates the total. "Make sure you keep some money in your pocket. You never know when you will need it."

Felicita doesn't take another bite, and Beto finishes the food on her plate.

Once Toño informs his family of his decision, he wants to leave as soon as possible. He goes over to his neighbor's house after dinner—she is one of the women who makes pupusas stuffed with loroco and sells them twice a week in the market— and she agrees to buy the plants but deducts the cost of the harvest. The plants still need a few more weeks until they are ready, and Toño won't be around to provide the labor.

Toño begins the process of selling the animals the next morning. When nobody in town expresses any interest in his bull, his cow, or his calf, he brings them to the market the following day. He sells the calf and the bull but has to bring the cow home.

"Did you sell the other two?" Felicita asks while Toño eats dinner alone. The rest of his family ate their meal hours before and are now out visiting friends.

"One farmer from San Vicente took them. I'll sell the cow tomorrow."

His mother nods and pulls out the ingredients necessary to prepare the dough for tomorrow's tortillas.

Toño counts his money after he finds a buyer for the cow in the market on Saturday and discovers he is still one thousand colones short of the ten thousand he needs to cross the border. The only possession he has left to sell is his half of the horse he shares with Beto.

"Will you buy my half of the horse from me?" Toño asks Beto while the two of them make the rounds of the family's farm Sunday morning before church. It's been three days since Toño announced his plan to leave, and in this short time the plants have exploded in size, color, and ripeness, as if the land is trying to convince Toño his place is here, with them.

"Why would I do that?" Beto says. He is the only one who ever uses the horse—Toño doesn't mind walking—and when Toño leaves it will be one hundred percent his.

"Because I won't be here to use my half. It's only fair."

"I'll give you one and a half thousand colones for it." The horse is worth four and both brothers know it.

"Two." Toño knows full well Beto doesn't have the money and will ask his dad for the cash. It wouldn't be the first time Jose Angel helps one of his sons with money and won't be the last.

"One point seven five."

"Two."

"Fine. Two." Beto says with a smile.

The two brothers shake hands and continue the inspection of their crops. As they reach the end of their property and turn around, ripened oranges, larger and more colorful than either brother has even seen, begin to drop down in front of them. At first they collect as much as they can, but soon they each have as much as they can carry and still the fruit drops down in front of them on their way back home.

"This is crazy!" Beto exclaims.

Toño looks up to see what could be causing so much fruit to drop, but there are no monkeys in the trees and there isn't any wind at all. A coconut begins to fall from overhead and Toño steps to the side, out of the way of the projectile. "Run!" he says.

The two brothers run through the coconut grove, arms full of oranges, without being struck by the falling drupes. They turn around beneath the banana trees and see stillness has returned to the trees they just passed beneath. Coconuts litter the footpath close by, oranges in the distance.

A banana falls from the tree above them.

"Let's grab Angel and Alfonso and pick up all this fruit," Beto says. "Too bad you're leaving tomorrow—if this keeps up we will have a lot of work to do!"

The trees hold their breath until they hear what Toño will say.

"Too bad," Toño says.

The oranges in the upturned shirts of the brothers begin to rot. By the time the brothers realize and drop their haul, their shirts are stained with foul-smelling juice. The husks of the coconuts on the ground crack open and spill their juice onto the earth.

Beto is crestfallen, his eyes searching for an explanation of what just happened.

Toño kicks the rotted oranges off the dirt path. "Let's get ready for church," he says.

CHAPTER EIGHT

EVERYONE BUT JOSE ANGEL shows up to church ten minutes before mass begins. Jose Angel hasn't been to church for as long as Toño can remember, but Felicita makes sure all her children show up each week with remote support from her husband.

Toño searches the entering families, looking for Hortensia. He hopes this isn't the rare service she attends. Each pair of bright red lips causes his heart to jump until, right before the service is about to begin, he spots her bright red lips enter the church. His heart leaps into his throat.

Hortensia's face lights up when she sees him, but she makes no outward sign in his direction. This is the first time they have seen each other in over a week.

Toño doesn't hear a single word the priest says over the next hour and a half.

Hortensia waits for Toño outside the church. "Toño!" she says when he walks into the sunlight.

Toño tells his family he will see them back at the house and walks towards the young woman.

Hortensia moves as if she will give Toño a hug, but both the public nature of their meeting and Toño's demeanor stop her in her tracks.

Toño gathers his strength to release the words he hoped he wouldn't have to say. "I'm going to America tomorrow."

"You're leaving?"

"Tomorrow."

"Why didn't you tell me?"

A torrent of words builds up inside of Toño and pushes against the backs of his teeth in an effort to escape.

"Do you really want to know?"

Hortensia nods with tears in her eyes.

"If I tell you, please remember that you asked. Do you still want to know?"

Wet strands of black hair stick to Hortensia's cheek as she nods again.

"I was thinking about it the other day. Really thinking about it. What would our future look like? Would we get married? Have kids?"

Hortensia looks at Toño, her eyes grateful for confirmation of her innermost thoughts.

"And where would we live? With my dad?" Toño points to his chest. "I don't have land. You don't have land. Why would I want to be poor with you. Like you." He shakes his head. "No, all you have to offer is what's between your legs. It's best for both of us if you forget about me and continue on with your life."

The red in Hortensia's lips and nails drains away, leaving the color of flesh in its place. She stares at him with confused eyes. "I have to tell you something too," she says. She takes a deep breath and says, "I was going to wait but it looks like I won't have another chance."

Hortensia pauses.

"What is it?"

"I'm pregnant," she says.

The words take a moment to sink in. Toño looks at her stomach, no larger than before. "So?" he says.

"It's yours."

"How am I supposed to know that? I don't know who you've been sleeping with." These words would have pierced her heart if Toño hadn't already ripped it out with his tongue.

"How can you say that?" Hortensia croaks. "All the time we spent together—"

"Is in the past," Toño finishes her sentence. "Look, there's a lot I have to do before I leave. Good luck to you and your baby."

Toño turns his back on Hortensia's muffled sobs. Her guts have been ripped out and spread on the grounds of the church for everyone to see. But she still has her legs. She turns and runs back home with a river of tears streaming from her face, enough to fill the ditches on both sides of the road and wash Toño's pile of rose petals away.

Toño spends the rest of Sunday with his family and doesn't pack his bag until Monday morning, the day he is scheduled to leave. His family pretends today is the same as every other day and busy themselves with their chores, but the heaviness of the air gives away their nervousness. Toño, for his part, knows he does a lot on the farm and feels bad the rest of the family will have to pick up the slack he leaves behind.

Toño feels eyes on the back of his head while he looks over the possessions he has decided to leave behind. He turns around and sees his mother standing in the doorway with tears in her eyes.

"You're really going, Toño?" she says.

"I'm really going," he says as he slings his backpack over his shoulders.

She lingers in the doorway, inspecting her second son,

looking as if she has more to say, but no more words come from her lips. Her words come out as tears streaming down her face. Toño is surprised to find that the words she leaves unsaid resonate in his heart, as if the tears have a language of their own. "You don't have to be scared for me. I told you I'm coming back!"

"But what if you don't? What if you meet a woman and fall in love and never come back?"

Toño crosses the room in three long strides and wraps his arms around his mother. Her tears soak the shoulders of his shirt.

Satisfied he has packed all he will need, Toño walks into the main room of the house, where his family have stopped their tasks in order to say goodbye. While he hugs his younger brothers and sisters he realizes Rosa is missing.

"Where's Rosa?" he says to Jose Angel.

"Ran off a few minutes ago," Alfonso says.

"Probably to find an anthill," Beto says with a chuckle.

When Rosa gets upset, she puts her bare feet into an anthill and lets the zompopo ants bite her feet. The bites stay red and swollen for days.

Felicita grabs a pot and begins to prepare the poultice that will bring the girl some semblance of relief.

Toño hugs Beto.

"My American brother," Beto says with a forced laugh.

The last person Toño says goodbye to is his father. They stand in front of each other for a long moment, each of them unsure of where to start.

"Let me walk with you," Jose Angel says.

Toño and his father walk to and through the market to where the bus will pick Toño up. They get there with plenty of time to spare before the bus leaves.

"I want you to know you always have a home to come back

to," Toño's father says, cold and emotionless, as if he is stating a fact. He pulls his wallet from his back pocket and holds out one thousand colones for his son in his stiff metal hands.

His father's words cause a lump to form in Toño's throat.

"No, I won't take your money," Toño manages to say.

"I want you to have some money in your pocket."

"I will. Tomas is fine with me paying him eight thousand colones. I'll keep the other two with me."

"He's fine with you getting the rest to him later?"

"He said I'll have a few months to earn the money and pay him back. I'd rather do it this way than cross into America without any money at all. Never know when you will need some money in your pocket."

Pride for his son causes Jose Angel to grow two inches taller, extra height that will take a year to recede. "You'll do great things in the United States."

The years in Jose Angel's face show up out of nowhere. The mask he wore had hidden the wrinkles at the corners of his eyes, his white hair, and the bald spot on his head. His skin becomes blotched with stains from years of labor in the sun.

Toño realizes what must be done while he watches his father age before his eyes. While he is in the United States, he must make enough money to expand upon what his father has built, not buy his own separate farm. More land and more resources so one day, far in the future, if his son wants to go to the university to become an agronomist, he will be able to pay for it. He doesn't want to become his own man; he wants to become his father's son.

The bus that will take Toño to meet Tomas in Mexico pulls up, chased by a cloud of black smoke. Toño and Jose Angel exchange an awkward hug, their first, and Toño boards the bus wondering how his years away will show up in his father's face when they see each other again.

PART 2

INTO THE FIRE

CHAPTER NINE

THE BUS DROPS Toño off in Tijuana after two days of travel through Guatemala, Oaxaca, and Mexico City. Toño stares with wide eyes at clogged streets full of yellow taxis and signs advertising everything from food to live sex shows littered along the sidewalk. Stray dogs and cats, some missing legs and all of them scarred, scavenge in forgotten corners.

Tomas said he would be at the Hotel de Valles, the address of which is written on a piece of paper in Toño's hand. All Toño has to do is "get his ass there." A young woman behind the ticketing counter tells Toño which way to walk, a straight shot down Calle Benito Juarez 2da.

The city blocks seem to go on forever. The spaces between streets present either a building's flat face with a solitary, metal-barred door or a metal fence with bars ten feet high. There are advertisements for lawyers, taxis, and more than one hotel with rates by the hour.

Sweat stains under Toño's armpits and neck darken his gray T-shirt by the time he gets to Hotel de Valles. His heart pounds, and Toño uses the bottom of his shirt to wipe his sweaty face. Toño walks inside, and the attendant in the front lobby doesn't bother to take his eyes off a telenovela on a small black-and-white screen.

Toño pulls a piece of paper from his pocket and checks which room he is supposed to go to: room 311. He remembers Tomas's instructions from their phone conversation. "Three knocks, three pauses, two knocks, two pauses, then one knock. Someone will ask for the password. Remember this and don't write it down: Sopa de mariscos."

The door to room 311 swings open and a dark-skinned Cuban asks for his name.

"Juan Antonio."

The Cuban's eyes narrow and he inspects Toño from head to toe. He holds out a hand and nods to the backpack, which Toño hands over. The Cuban looks through Toño's belongings while Toño stands still, unsure of what to do.

A toilet flushes somewhere inside the room and Tomas walks in front of the open door, wiping his hands on his pants. "Toño! You made it," he says. Tomas walks forward and taps the Cuban on the shoulder. "Relax, Gustavo, he's family."

The inspector grunts and throws all of Toño's clothes back into the backpack, no longer folded and organized.

The three men spend the afternoon drinking beers and talking. Gustavo works with Tomas as a pollero, a chicken herder, and they refer to Toño as their pollo. One more pollo is scheduled to get to the hotel the next day, so the rest of their day is wide open while they wait. Their plan is to cross the border by night with two other polleros and their pollos to rendezvous with the drivers who will pick them all up.

The other pollo never shows up. The three men wait in room 311 all day before Tomas announces they'll leave without him.

Toño is shaken awake at three in the morning. "It's time to go," Tomas says, the smell of alcohol heavy on his breath. Who else could charge an arm and a leg to complete a job and show up drunk?

Gustavo thrusts a cup of coffee into Toño's hand. "Drink," he commands. The coffee is room temperature and mixed with whiskey. Toño empties the cup in three large swigs.

Before Toño can process their situation the three men have left the hotel. Tomas walks in front of Toño and the Cuban behind. The closer they get to the border, the slower their travel becomes. Each city block turns into a sprint before they wait in dark alleys for helicopters to pass by overhead. Hours pass by before the three men climb under a fence outside the city. Toño stands tall and inhales the air in what he presumes to be the United States.

"Not that easy, amigo, we still need to get across the river," Tomas says. He and Gustavo break into a run. Toño chases them down and all three of them manage to swim across.

Dripping wet, but in America, they walk to the entrance of a sewer. Tomas tells Gustavo to remove the manhole cover. The three men are then greeted by the smell of human excrement. They wait in the dark covered by the stench, just below the manhole cover, for half an hour before the other two polleros show up. One has three pollos, the other four. Some of the pollos look scared, some excited, but all of them disgusted by the smell in their nostrils and the brown liquid covering their feet.

The group trudges through the waste for most of an hour. Twice, Toño steps on something hard and almost falls each time before he regains his footing.

"Careful, amigo, you don't want to get your hands in this stuff," Tomas says.

Toño nods in agreement but doesn't say a word to avoid adding his own vomit to the mixture below.

The group spots an X spray-painted in white on the wall opposite a metal ladder. "This is us," Tomas says.

Gustavo is the first up the ladder. He raises the manhole cover and peers into the darkness outside before he throws the cover off and climbs out of the sewer. The rest of the men follow. Toño exhales the putrid air from his lungs and stomps his feet on the asphalt to kick off as much of the sewage as he can.

The men gather next to a nearby warehouse. A white van and a red sports car idle close by, their headlights pointed at the men.

"Isn't there supposed to be one more?" a man yells from the light.

"They never showed," Tomas yells back.

The driver of the sports car, a military man with a short crew cut and ramrod-straight posture, wants all of the travelers to ride in the van, but they won't all be able to fit. "No way you're sitting in my car, you smell like shit," he says.

"Why'd you bring this car? You knew how we would cross," Tomas fires back.

"I can take two, but you'll have to ride in the trunk."

"You're the one without all your pollos, you should have to ride in there," one of the other polleros tells Toño. In the light, Toño can see his scarred face and massive forearms.

Tomas is silent for a moment. "Fine," he says. "Me and Toño will do it." He gestures for the rest of the group to come over to the two vehicles.

Tomas and Gustavo shake hands before Gustavo gives Toño a nod goodbye. The Cuban climbs into the van. The driver of the van is a Chicano and has brought a woman along, a white woman with short blond hair.

Toño and Tomas get into the rear of the sports car. "This shit smell better come out," the military man says before he slams the trunk shut. They are in the trunk for no more than half an hour before the sound of sirens can be heard outside.

"Immigration! Pull over!"

The car slows down and comes to a stop. Sounds of chaos and multiple sets of hurried footsteps can be heard from outside. "Stop!" the officers yell.

The footsteps drown away and two voices are heard from outside the sports car.

"Who drove the van?" an officer asks in Spanish.

"I don't know. I was on my way home after work when you pulled me over," the military man says.

"Were you now? And those are your worn-out bags in the back seat too?"

The sound of the military man thrust onto the hood of the car reaches the two men still inside.

"With any luck they won't look in the trunk," Tomas whispers.

These words are out in the world for less than a moment before a key unlocks the trunk. It pops open and Toño is blinded by the sudden brightness of a flashlight shining into his eyes.

"What do we have here? Get out, you two!"

Tomas and Toño climb out of the car. The van is ahead of the sports car, empty. Everyone else has run away.

"Shit," the military man mutters as he looks away from the two men who have been pulled from the trunk of his car.

Toño begins to laugh and can't stop.

"Shh! Keep quiet! You'll get us in trouble!" Tomas hisses.

Toño's laughter intensifies. He has no fear of these men. This is just an adventure! He knows he can always go back to his father's home. These serious men don't realize how inconsequential their jobs are.

The military man tells the officers his tale. "Look, I'll level with you. After I crossed the border, the driver of the van told me to drive this car. Said to keep these two in the trunk, instead of in the back, so nobody would be suspicious. I've always wanted to come to America . . ." he says, his voice trailing away, a faraway look in his eyes.

Toño is almost convinced. In another life this man could have acted on TV.

"Is that so?" the officer says. "Who's in charge then?"

"I don't know, their face was hidden."

The officer turns his face to Tomas and a laughing Toño. "Who brought you over here? Was it him?" He points to the man in handcuffs pinned to the hood of the car.

"I don't know," Tomas says.

The officer taps the pollero on the shoulder, a gesture both reassuring and ominous, and turns to Toño.

"All right, giggles, who brought you over here?"

Toño tries to pull himself together before he answers. "We were drinking in Tijuana, having a good time, and walked by this car. The trunk was open so we got in!"

The officer stares at Toño for a long time before a thin smile spreads across his lips, uncovering deep lines around tired eyes. He turns back to his vehicle and addresses a fellow officer. "Take 'em back to Mexico!"

"What about the driver?"

"What about him? They're Mexico's problem now."

More officers return from the night, their bodies materializing from the edge of the circle of lights from the vehicles. The others were able to get away. The officers never thought to take a closer look at the dozen or so chickens next to piles of discarded clothes.

CHAPTER TEN

THE LARGE DOOR that separates the United States from Mexico swings open and the three men are thrown across the border in the early-morning sun. Dozens of yellow taxis in various stages of disrepair wait to take those on foot to their destinations in Tijuana. Tomas hails one of the taxis and tells the driver to take them back to the Hotel de Valles.

"How did you think of that?" Tomas asks Toño on their ride back to the hotel.

"Think of what?" Toño replies.

"That we saw the open trunk and climbed in!"

The military man reaches across Tomas and slaps Toño twice on the knee. "Quick thinking, amigo!"

"I don't know, I thought it was funny. They were so serious!"

"Americans are like that. They don't like us. Never will," Tomas says.

Toño decides to keep his distance from Americans once he makes it into their country, so they won't have a reason to kick him out again.

The cab drops the three men off outside the hotel and the

military man leaves Toño and Tomas, telling them to go with God. The two men get a room and sleep until the early afternoon before they wake up and find a bar to grab a drink at Tomas's insistence. Tomas places a phone call to schedule them to cross the border in two days.

For Toño, this extra time means he has to find a way to feed himself for the least possible cost. His diet consists of bread, beans, and, once a day, cheese.

Tomas lives like he is on vacation. He doesn't eat much because he prefers to drink his calories. From his morning beer to when he switches to liquor at dinner, he is never sober. Tomas doesn't talk about his wife, Toño's cousin Dolores, and, from what Toño can tell, doesn't bother to call her. From the way Tomas acts there is no indication he is even married. He makes sure not to talk about other women in front of Toño, but where else could a man be when he doesn't get back until two in the morning, long after Toño has gone to bed, with a wide, satisfied grin on his face and the smell of sweat and body fluids dripping from his pores?

The day of their departure arrives, and Toño finds out they are the only two who need to cross.

"Since we don't have a large group with us it doesn't make sense to go through the tunnel," Tomas tells Toño.

"Lead the way," Toño says, tired of wasting time in the Mexican border town. The past two days have been a unique form of hell; he is used to waking up early and being busy all day. All he thinks about is the money to be made in America.

The two men approach the border the same way they did before: sprint one block, wait, sprint, wait. Helicopters pass by overhead but this time with greater frequency, as if they know Toño is about to make his second attempt to enter the United States and are hell-bent on making sure he doesn't. The two men end up next to a tall fence at the edge of the city. They find a spot where a hole has been dug underneath and cross to the other side. They swim across the river. This time, instead of going into the sewer, the two men run into the hills of the American Southwest.

If Tomas wasn't sure of the way, Toño would have gotten lost in the expanse. The ground is rocky and seems to repeat itself as it stretches away into the pitch-black night. Tomas doesn't need a flashlight and relies on his memory to navigate. The two men walk for hours. Toño's stomach reminds him he needs to eat, but he calms the organ with assurances of food from wherever they end up. He has heard about the grocery stores in this country, how they have everything one could ever hope for waiting on shelves, and he can't wait to see for himself if the rumors are true.

A rattlesnake warns the travelers about their proximity to her nest while Toño dreams about the type of meat he wants to eat for breakfast. Her rattle shakes the cold night air and condensation coalesces into ice crystals, freezing both Tomas and Toño in their tracks.

"Do you see where it is?" Tomas says through clenched teeth.

"Not yet," Toño says. Eyeballs in frozen sockets scan their immediate surroundings to make sure they aren't in striking distance.

The rattle continues and the rocks around the men begin to vibrate. Toño spots the snake three paces away and off to the right. He manages to pry himself free from his frozen state, pick up a large rock, and creep forward. When he is close enough to not miss, but not close enough to be bitten, he drops the rock on her head. The night thaws and stillness returns to the rocks.

"What'd you do that for?" Tomas asks him.

"You have to kill a snake when you see it," Toño replies, echoing the words of his father.

Tomas shakes his head and resumes their trek. "She was nice enough to warn us. We could have kept walking."

Toño shrugs and follows in Tomas's footsteps. It takes them until dawn to get to the van waiting for them. Inside is the Chicano and his American woman.

"Good to see you again, compadre," Tomas says as he and Toño climb into the back seat.

"Good to see you without the smell of shit in my nostrils," the Chicano replies. Toño and the woman stay silent, but she stares at Toño through the passenger-side mirror.

Tomas taps Toño on the thigh. "Welcome to America! Let's have a drink to celebrate." The Chicano passes back a six-pack of beers in a plastic bag and the two men drink in the back seat.

The Chicano drives for hours while the sun rises over the horizon, taking Toño and Tomas all the way to Los Angeles.

Manuel had given Toño his address before he left El Salvador. The Chicano weaves through the city streets on the way to Manuel's apartment. He interrupts Toño's thoughts of how so many people could live in one place to point out the Hollywood sign on the mountain in the distance. Toño leans forward to look through the windshield, shrugs when he sees the sign, and leans back into his ruminations.

"It's famous," Tomas informs his pollo after he notices Toño's lack of appreciation.

When Toño is dropped off at his destination, he says goodbye to Tomas with promises to pay his remaining balance off in the near future.

"Once you get a job, give me a call and we can settle up," Tomas says from inside the van. He closes the door and the Chicano drives away, the woman's eyes still rooted on Toño through her mirror.

The key to get into the apartment was left with a neighbor, an old woman who has spent so much time with her cats that Manuel says she has grown whiskers herself. Toño knocks on her door while preparing to act like he doesn't see anything out of the ordinary. The door opens, and not only does the neighbor have thin feline whiskers around her mouth, but her eyes have also transformed to slits and the bridge of her nose has all but disappeared. Two cats slink around behind her in the shadows of the apartment. With a purr, she hands over Manuel's key and licks the back of one hand while she uses the other to close her door without a word being said.

Manuel lives with his brother Jorge in a one-bedroom apartment on the second floor. Toño lets himself in and finds a solitary couch, a small TV, and a coffee table with one leg propped up by a stack of magazines. Leftover bottles of Coca-Cola and old takeout containers litter the counters, and the trash needs to be emptied.

Toño sets his bag down on the couch and walks into the bedroom to inspect the closet where he was informed he will sleep. The closet is empty, save for a few shirts on hangers, and just long enough for him to lie down.

Manuel is the first of the brothers to get home. He walks in the front door just after four in the afternoon. When he sees Toño he flashes a bright white smile, tosses his bag down next to Toño's on the couch, and embraces his old friend.

"Toño! Did you have any trouble finding the place?" he says when they separate. He ends the statement with a click of his teeth, a quirk Toño had forgotten about.

"None at all," Toño says. "You said your neighbor had whiskers, but you never mentioned she's almost turned into a cat!" Toño says with a laugh.

"I told you! No surprise, she spends enough time with those animals."

Toño looks around the room again, this time seeing it with

his friend's eyes. "Thanks for letting me stay here. Is Jorge still at work?"

"He doesn't get home until seven each night. On Fridays I usually get home around then too, but I came home early because I knew you were here."

Toño fishes the key from his pocket and holds it out for Manuel.

"You keep it, I never use it."

"You never lock the door?"

"No, we lock it every time, I just don't need the key. I trained the lock to open when I click my teeth," Manuel says, as if this is the most natural thing in the world.

CHAPTER ELEVEN

JORGE GETS home at seven on the dot and the three ex-neighbors stay up late catching up over beers and takeout Chinese food.

"Remember that time the other team chased us with machetes?" Jorge says after Manuel brings up their time playing soccer together. The two brothers look nothing alike, Manuel long and thin and Jorge short, stocky, and overweight. Jorge's smile is wide but nowhere near as brilliant as his brother's.

Toño and Manuel both laugh. "Those guys never gave us our money back!" says Toño.

"We would have beat them too!" Manuel adds, his words clipped by his white teeth.

"We? Who's we? You never saw the field," Jorge says, his words hard and sharp.

Toño laughs to try and blunt the statement.

Manuel was a permanent substitute and never saw the field. He stares at his brother with his eyes full of pain from the picked-off scab.

Toño knows this argument has been scratched at before; he has been present for many previous iterations, and who knows how many times the brothers have brought it up without any witnesses.

"You're right, we would have won!" Toño says, agreeing with Manuel. "I'm going to grab another beer, either of you want one?"

"I'll take one," Jorge says with a cheerful smile.

"No thanks, I'm good," Manuel says. He tries his best to hide the sour look, but his expressive face is too easy to read. "I'm going to bed."

"Don't be like that," Jorge says.

Manuel sulks into the back bedroom.

"Such a baby," Jorge says as he cracks open the beer handed to him by Toño. Manuel takes the conversation to bed with him and the two men spend the rest of the night watching American sitcoms. Jorge finishes the six-pack alone and both he and Toño try their best to understand the English-language show more than they already do.

Toño spends the rest of the weekend with the brothers, learning about the neighborhood and spending more money on food than he is comfortable with. He finds out Manuel's job is to assemble gold chains, and his friend promises to teach Toño to do the same. Each week, Manuel picks up the bag of gold links on Monday, assembles them into chains at the apartment Tuesday through Thursday, and drops off his completed work on Friday. He gets paid based on the length of chain he is able to produce.

Manuel brings Toño with him to the jewelry store on Monday. The owner of the store, a Jewish man named Coleman, sells products in two different locations. His flagship store in Hollywood is where he spends most of his time, while his wife and eldest son manage the Inglewood location.

A bell rings out as they walk through the front door.

"Hey boss, I have another worker for you," Manuel tells the

store owner. "He worked with gold back in El Salvador and he said he would be happy to work for you now that he is living in the States," Manuel says in English.

Toño is amazed at how well his friend can speak the language after less than a year in the United States. His own tongue doesn't like speaking in English, but his ears are able to comprehend most of what is said as long as the speaker doesn't rush their words. Toño opens his mouth to disagree with Manuel's claim about his level of experience, but Manuel's confidence stifles his voice.

Coleman looks at Toño through his jeweler's loupe, sizes him up in less than a second, and shrugs. His bald head reflects the bright lights overhead and his eyes have a permanent squint from a lifetime spent staring at the shine given off by his jewels. "He can start with half as much as I give you," he says.

Manuel puts their gold links into a backpack he brought just for this purpose and they leave the store. "Let's grab lunch for later before we get to work," Manuel says as they walk down the sidewalk.

"I've never worked with gold before," Toño tells Manuel.

"Oh well, he doesn't know that!"

"He will when we turn in the chain on Friday," Toño replies.

"How can he know that? Even if you're slow you should be able to get all your work done; you only have half as much as me."

"If you say so."

"Where do you want to eat?" Manuel asks.

"McDonald's," says Toño without hesitation.

They get hamburgers to go, and when they get back to the apartment they put them in the refrigerator before they get ready for the day's work. They clear the coffee table of the empty beer bottles from the weekend and each take a spot on the couch. Once Manuel teaches Toño how to get started, the two men work in silence, absorbed in the assembly.

The work is tedious. Small links need to be arranged in a spiral one link at a time with the next links providing the tension so individual components don't spin and become unattached. Toño is able to get a tentative rhythm of the work down within the first hour, but his pace isn't even close to how fast Manuel is able to assemble his chains. His friend is able to watch TV while his hands do the work for him. Manuel's pile of gold links seem to prefer being among their friends in the chain and swarm together in the correct pattern as if they are magnetized.

"How long does each chain have to be?" Toño asks during their lunch break. He has produced one foot of chain and looks at the five his friend has been able to produce.

"As long as we can make it," Manuel says before he washes down a bite of hamburger with a sip of Coke.

"What happens if they don't need it so long?"

"Then they cut it."

Toño looks at his chain, wondering how the process would work.

"Yes, they cut it and attach an end piece. The extra links get tossed back into the scrap heap and melted down to make more links later." Manuel has a habit of making everything sound simple.

When Jorge gets home, Manuel tells Toño their work for the day is done. Toño has been able to assemble three feet of chain to Manuel's ten. Toño wonders if Manuel decides to eat lunch after the first five feet of chain and wraps up the day after the second five but doesn't want to ask.

Toño goes to the bathroom and comes back out to find Jorge eating dinner alone on the couch in the same spot Toño spent all day working. Manuel informs Toño he will make food for the both of them, and Toño can't help but wonder why the brothers wouldn't take turns making dinner for each other.

Once dinner—white rice and black beans—is ready, Manuel retakes his own spot on the couch next to his brother, and Toño eats his meal standing up at the counter.

"We can figure out how to split the grocery bill later," Manuel says through a mouthful of food. A look of disgust flashes across Jorge's face before Toño can agree to the arrangement.

Manuel's eyes are glued to the television and he doesn't notice his older brother's reaction. Jorge's eyes scream "woman," like Manuel has some sort of feminine quality that he should be ashamed of.

The look in the older brother's eyes isn't directed at Toño, but it manages to be the last thing he thinks of before falling asleep and the first thing he remembers when he wakes up the next morning. He wonders if those eyes were with him through the previous night, but since he never remembers his dreams, and therefore assumes he has none, he decides it isn't possible.

CHAPTER TWELVE

AT ONE POINT during production on Tuesday, Toño's hands take over the work while Toño reminisces about life on the farm in El Salvador. When he realizes his hands are working on their own, the spell is broken, and the assembled links split apart. Toño is able to finish his day's five feet an hour after lunch. He places his hands on his knees and stands up. "I'll be back," he tells Manuel.

Manuel grunts and his eyes stay glued to the television.

Toño walks down the block to the grocery store and buys bananas, chocolate chip cookies, and instant coffee for his breakfasts and bread, peanut butter, and cheese for his dinners. He's grateful for the help Manuel has provided, but he doesn't want to impose. On his walk back, he takes a bent folding chair from a pile of trash so he has somewhere to sit when Jorge is home and they all want to watch TV.

Manuel is upset when Toño shows up with his own food. "What did you do that for?"

"I don't want you to have to feed me, I'll feed myself."

"You didn't like dinner?"

"I'll pay you for that too."

"Don't be ridiculous! What's gotten into you?"

Toño doesn't have the words to explain his reason. Even an attempt at vocalizing his feelings about Jorge's reaction would hurt his friend, so he decides to say nothing at all.

Toño is able to produce six feet of chain on Wednesday, Thursday, and Friday to make up for the two feet of gold chain he missed during Monday's production. Coleman inspects the seventy-five feet of gold chain—fifty from Manuel and twenty five from Toño—at the jewelry store on Friday and concludes they are satisfactory. The two friends leave with cash in hand and return home after a quick stop for hamburgers at McDonald's.

"Time to get ready for my date!" Manuel says the moment they walk through the door.

Toño has been hearing about this date all week. The woman, Lenore, is from El Salvador. She has been denying Manuel's request to take her out to dinner for months but for some reason said yes when Manuel called to ask her again this week. Manuel, who was expecting another no, is convinced Toño is his lucky charm and insists on taking a possession of Toño's with him tonight.

"I don't have anything for you to take!" Toño says with a laugh as Manuel closes the bathroom door.

"There has to be something," Manuel says when he walks back out after his shower, drying his hair with a threadbare white towel.

Toño looks through his possessions on the floor of the closet. He digs through his bag while Manuel gets dressed, looking for a small something that Manuel could stick in his pocket, and finds nothing.

"What if I give you money," Toño suggests.

"Money! I already have money, we got paid today."

"But it would be my money. I owe you for dinner the other night anyways."

"Then wouldn't it be my money?"

Toño ponders the question. "Good point," he says.

Manuel slides a watch over his wrist. "Do you have a ring or a necklace?"

Toño shakes his head; he's always found jewelry useless.

"You could wear my socks. They're clean, I promise."

"Socks! You don't have anything else?"

"I just got here last week! All I have is my backpack and the clothes I wore."

Manuel begins to fix his hair and Toño is taken back to the bathroom in the schoolhouse, when he combed his hair before graduating. He reaches into his back pocket and takes out his plastic comb, missing two teeth.

"Take this," Toño says as he hands it to Manuel.

"Perfect!" Manuel inspects the comb before using it to slick back his hair. He turns around and presents himself to Toño. "How do I look?"

"Look like you're ready to have a good night," Toño says with a wink.

Manuel leaves Toño alone in the apartment. He puts his feet on the coffee table and watches the news on the only Spanish-language channel available. Warm feelings of accomplishment for making it to America wash over him without anyone there to distract his thoughts. None of the broadcaster's words reach his ears, and he doesn't hear about the rotten fruit that has shown up in every corner of his home country.

Toño is asleep on the couch, the television still on, when Manuel and Lenore come storming through the door of the apartment, drunk. Manuel introduces his lady to his friend before Lenore excuses herself to use the restroom.

Manuel sits down on the couch and throws an arm around

Toño. "It worked!" he says. His breath reeks of liquor, his clothes are disheveled, but his hair is as perfect as when he left.

Toño is happy for his friend and doesn't mind being woken up. "I see that! You'll have some fun tonight."

"Thanks again, my friend. My lucky charm! You'll have to sleep on the couch tonight." The only downside to living in a one-bedroom apartment.

"Of course, of course. Thank goodness Jorge isn't here or else I'd have to sleep on the floor!"

Manuel leads Lenore into the bedroom as soon as she reemerges. The next morning, she leaves, telling Toño it was nice to meet him. Two weeks later, she leaves in the morning saying, "Good to see you again!" and every Saturday morning after that she asks about Toño's plans for the weekend before cooking the three of them breakfast.

The first Saturday night Lenore spends the night, a month and a half after her first date with Manuel, she invites Toño to mass the next morning.

"I go every Sunday," she informs him. "Manuel already said he's coming and we thought you might like to come! We'll get lunch somewhere after."

Toño hasn't been to a worship service since he left El Salvador and his chest tightens at the thought of going back, guilt for being away. "I'd love to! I used to go every Sunday with my mom."

"Oh really?" Lenore says. She turns to Manuel. "You didn't tell me he went to church every Sunday!"

"I didn't know," Manuel says from the couch. "He hasn't been since he's been here."

"There are some women who might want to meet you," Lenore says with a mischievous grin.

Toño agrees to meet the women, curious if any of them will be the right fit. When Manuel and Lenore leave for dinner,

Toño stays awake for a while longer wondering what would happen if both he and Manuel brought a woman back. And if Jorge decides to bring someone back the same night? Things could get interesting with the ornery brother. Luckily for all involved, he spends his weekends at his woman's place, away from the shrinking apartment.

CHAPTER THIRTEEN

THE INVITATION to church is the first in a series of invitations, the most recent of which is to a birthday party for Lenore's friend from work. Toño has tried to make new friends among the other Salvadoran transplants he has met, but so far he has been unable to expand his social circle beyond Manuel.

Toño is worried there will be a lot of Americans at the party. Both Manuel and Lenore have no problem speaking English, so on the ride there he flexes his tongue in every angle he can imagine to keep it loose in order to use what little parts of the language he knows.

The gathering is held on the patio of a house on the outskirts of the city. Rumor has it the neighbors have been paid to ignore the noise from the DJ, who is slated to play until four in the morning. The familiar rhythm of Spanish music finds Toño as he approaches the house, and when he enters he is delighted to find a room full of people who share his skin tone.

Toño begins the night with a beer. In his past life, in a small town in El Salvador where everyone knows who you are, he would stick with a few drinks over the course of a night. Tonight he finds himself thirstier than he has ever been before, the anonymity sucking all the liquid from his body, and his hand is never empty. By the time he meets a young woman with a hometown near his own, he has enough beers in his system to get rid of any inhibitions he harbors about making small talk. This far away from El Salvador, the two of them can consider themselves neighbors.

"My brother is looking at a house there," Toño tells her. The last time he spoke to his mother on the phone, she mentioned that Beto is looking to move sometime within the next few months.

"Oh really? He would be lucky to get it, it's a wonderful town."

"Can't be as wonderful as San Ramon!"

They stand next to each other in silence, their heads moving in time with the music. "Do you dance?" she asks.

He doesn't, but the beer answers for him. "Of course I do!" Toño says.

The pair walk onto the dance floor, each with a beer in hand. Two songs later, Toño or the beer decides it's time to make a move. "Would you want to go out with me?" he says.

"Go out? We are out!" she says with a laugh.

"You know what I mean," Toño says, getting serious.

The woman's torso stops moving but her hips keep the rhythm of the beat. "No, no, no, my friend. You don't get it that way with me!"

She leaves Toño on the dance floor, throws her empty can away, and goes to the table of drinks to get herself another. Toño, not to be shaken off, follows her. "What do you mean?" he says.

The woman reaches into the cooler and pulls out a bottled beer. "I don't like Salvadoran men."

"Oh really? Why?"

"Too machista."

Toño has never heard this word before and wonders why the description is applied to all men from his country. "What do you mean?" he says. He finishes his beer and tosses the empty can in the trash.

"You know what I mean! The woman has to do everything . . . cook for them, clean for them, wash their clothes, iron. Not the type of man I want." She looks at Toño from head to toe. "No offense," she says.

"I do all that stuff myself!"

"That's because you're single. Wait, as soon as you get a woman you'll expect her to take care of you just like your mamá back in San Ramon!"

Toño grabs the bottle of beer from her hand and twists the top off before handing it back to her. "Fuck you," he says. He doesn't say it to be mean, or even because he wants to fuck her; he says it because, deep down, he knows there's some truth to her words.

The woman ignores Toño's attack. "Can you speak English?" she asks before taking a sip of beer.

"Not yet."

"Do you have your green card?"

"No." Toño's face flushes with anger. "Why does it matter?"

"I could have stayed in El Salvador and found a man like you."

Toño walks away and doesn't talk to the woman for the rest of the night. He tries his luck with a few other women at the party but isn't able to engage in any worthwhile conversations after they find out he is from El Salvador. It's as if the woman who rejected him was able to whisper to all the women of the party to pass on this one specific immigrant. Instead of drinking the night away, Toño switches to water in an attempt to sober up before he heads home.

Manuel and Lenore notice their friend alone and walk over. They have been dancing all night and both their shirts are stuck to their chests with sweat.

"What's wrong?" Lenore asks.

"Nothing," Toño says. "I'm ready to leave when you are."

"Did you get any numbers?" Manuel says, scanning the women in the room.

"No, the one I talked to isn't interested in an immigrant."

"She said that? We're all immigrants!" Manuel says, surprised.

"She asked if I had my green card."

Manuel throws his arm around Lenore. "These women need to remember where they came from!" He asks Lenore if she's ready to go.

Lenore finishes her drink and nods.

Over the summer, at future parties he attends with Manuel and Lenore, Toño learns other Salvadoran women share the same sentiments about Salvadoran men without green cards. Too machista and not worth their time.

"No thanks," each woman would say when asked on a date, flattered but determined to keep Toño at a distance.

Toño learns to brush off the denials, to pretend he doesn't care, but deep down he wants to interrogate the women on their reasons in order to figure out what's wrong with him. He has a hard time understanding these women want a stable future in America, a future as a citizen but not as an immigrant. He comes to hate the concept of a green card and all it implies. He continues to cook, clean, and wash his clothes for himself in order to prove to himself he isn't too machista.

His problems would be solved if he was able to lie. No

70

woman ever asks to see official documentation, so whenever he is asked if he has a green card, he could just say "yes." But saying yes would imply he is in America for the long haul, that he isn't moving back after five years of work, and he isn't able to betray his homeland, even with items as small as words.

CHAPTER FOURTEEN

On a Monday in the spring of 1980, on their way to the jewelry store, Manuel tells Toño about an idea he says has "been on his mind for the past few days." "What do you know about New York?" he says.

"Nothing," Toño admits.

"Well you've heard of it, right? You know it's a city?"

"On the other side of the country. One of the biggest cities in the world."

"So you do know something about it!"

"I guess I do. Why do you ask?"

Manuel hesitates before he continues. "I want to move there. That's where my future lies, I know it."

Toño digests his friend's words, imagining life alone with Jorge if Manuel left.

"Do you want to come with me?" Manuel asks.

"Sure," Toño says. "Is Lenore coming too?"

"That's part of the reason I want to move. If I leave and still want her then I know she's the one."

"Does she know about this test?"

"I haven't told her yet. I wanted to see if you'd come with me."

Toño nods. They pick up their gold links—they now receive the same amount of work each week—and continue the conversation back outside.

"What if you decide you want her back but she doesn't want you?"

"Then I'll know she isn't the one."

"If you're sure about this . . ."

"I'm sure," Manuel says.

Toño and Manuel circle the end of the following week for their move. The week's order is larger than usual and they spend twelve hours each day, fourteen on Thursday, working in order to finish. In the end they are able to get their work done Thursday night and take the finished product to Coleman to get paid first thing Friday morning.

The Friday of their departure descends upon the two friends the way a sudden storm churns calm waters. Their lives in Los Angeles have never been better, more established, or more fulfilling. It's only because they are about to leave that the appreciation for their current situation comes to the forefront of their consciousness and they each realize how much they will miss California in their own way.

Their bus is set to depart at nine. The sun is up, and the two friends are excited for the trip. Jorge accompanies them to the bus depot to see them off.

"Did you figure out where you are going to live?" Manuel asks his older brother.

"I'll move in with Dolores." Dolores moved to Los Angeles after divorcing the pollero Tomas, and Toño introduced her to Jorge. The two have been in a relationship for months.

"Well, the rest of the month is paid for," Toño says. He and

Manuel have paid their share of the rent for the remaining two weeks.

"Is that all you have?" Jorge asks Toño. If either of the friends recognize the contempt in his voice, they don't act like it.

"This is all I need!" Toño says with pride. He doesn't need, or want, much, in case he decides to go back home.

Manuel stashes his luggage under the bus before awkward hugs are exchanged with Jorge. The two adventurers board the bus with their backpacks.

"I can't believe all these people came to say goodbye!" Manuel says with a laugh. He stands and looks out the window and pretends everyone who is here to say goodbye to the other passengers are here to say goodbye to him. "Goodbye everybody!" he says with a wave.

Toño laughs. "You're crazy!"

Manuel sits back down in his chair with a wide grin on his face. "Ready to start a new life?" he says.

"Ready!" Toño says. Nobody asked him this question when he came to America, but if they had, the answer would have been the same.

The bus stops twice a day on the trip across the country. Most times it stops at a McDonald's, but a few times, over long stretches of road with nothing but land extending miles into the distance, they stop at a rest stop. All of the passengers make sure to get out and stretch their legs even if they don't want to buy anything or have to use the restroom.

Toño sees snow for the first time at a McDonald's in Amarillo, Texas. The bus has pulled into the parking lot while he dozed, and Manuel shakes him awake to go inside and get food. Toño, his eyes still puffy, looks at the white substance around the half-covered parking lot.

"They forgot to rinse," he says. He wipes the sleep from his eyes with the backs of his hands.

"What did you say?" asks Manuel.

"Nothing."

Toño assumes the snow around the edges of the parking lot is leftover suds from someone scrubbing the parking lot clean. He has heard everything is bigger in Texas, so he looks for the giant who is responsible for keeping the parking lots clean or their giant push broom.

Manuel asks Toño for his order while they wait in line. A sign for a Big Mac catches Toño's eye and he tells Manuel to order him one. If he is honest with himself, he would realize he is attracted to the fact that both words in the name are easy to pronounce. Even though he has no problem pronouncing these two words, he still relays his order through Manuel.

If Toño decides on what to eat because of the simplicity of the name, then Manuel decides based on complexity. Manuel orders the most difficult-sounding item on the menu for the chance to acclimate his tongue to the demands of the English language. After he orders Toño's Big Mac, with large fries and a Coke, he orders himself a Quarter Pounder with cheese, medium fries, and a large Coke, unsatisfied by the lack of challenge provided by any of the other menu items. The two friends get their food and sit down in a booth next to the window.

"Someone should rinse the parking lot," Toño says between bites.

"What are you talking about?" asks Manuel. He follows Toño's gaze and sees the dirty snow in piles around the edges of the parking lot. He looks back at Toño, takes one look at the seriousness of his friend's face, and realizes Toño isn't joking. "That's snow!" Manuel cries out.

"Snow?" Toño has never seen it before. The places he's been have no business to conduct with snow, but then again, Texas in April should have no business with snow either.

Manuel is facedown with his head in the crook of his elbow.

His upper back shakes with laughter and Toño has to grab both drinks before the vibrations tip them over. He lifts his head with tears in his eyes. "Rinse? Did you think it was soap?"

Toño's face is red with embarrassment, but he can't help but join in his friend's laughter. Through a toothy grin he nods and manages to utter, "Yes!" He collects himself and asks Manuel when he's seen snow before. His question isn't an attack, more of a simple curiosity born from the fact Manuel has spent his life in the same climates as himself.

"I haven't but I recognized it!" Manuel says, shaking his head.

The two friends manage to finish their lunch through occasional fits of laughter. By the end of their meal both pairs of cheeks ache and there are no more tears left in their eyes.

They walk over to the edge of the parking lot when they leave the restaurant. The snow is dirt, packed down, and rounded from where the plows have pushed it into a pile. Toño picks up a frozen brick, more ice than snow, and smashes it on the asphalt. Manuel kicks the pile and exposes soft powder underneath. He tries to make a snowball, but it crumbles from his hands as soon as it's formed.

The bus driver honks twice to let the two men, and the rest of the passengers still in the restaurant, know it is time for them to get back on the road. This isn't his first time transporting immigrants cross-country, and he smiles every time he sees people experience snow for the first time. Most people see their first snow when they get to the East Coast, closer to New York, and more than once he has taught a kid how to make their first snowball.

As the bus pulls out of the parking lot, the giant responsible for snow removal walks from behind the restaurant to finish the work he started before it was time to take his break.

CHAPTER FIFTEEN

THE MIDDLE of the country passes by outside Toño's window. He finds it hard to believe there is so much land, and estimating the number of people it takes to work the land makes his head spin. If he ever needs to return to farming he knows all he would have to do is come back to this land and there would be work, but this isn't the kind of work he wants. The rest of his life in El Salvador will be spent on a farm. Here, in America, there are other ways to make money, ways that aren't tied to market prices and crop yields.

Toño and Manuel sleep on the bus, use the restroom on the bus, and relax on the bus between stops. In the morning on the third day of their trip, the passenger behind them leans forward and points to skyscrapers in the distance. "There's the city," she says.

The bus drops the passengers off at Grand Central Station. Compared to Los Angeles, with its open spaces and sunny atmosphere, New York City has a worn, frayed feel. If Toño had been a student of history he would know the city was over two hundred years older than Los Angeles, plenty of time for its inhabitants to rub up against the seams and wear down the stitching. The towering buildings are all a dull gray, a fact accentuated by the weaker sun in this part of the country. Trash covers the ground, solitary pieces blowing in the wind and stationary piles held down by their collective weight. Homeless people outside the bus station are somehow more threadbare, their edges less defined, than the ones Toño encountered on the other side of the country. How are there so many of them? Even Toño has heard about how cold the city can get.

Manuel gathers his luggage from beneath the bus and looks around. "We made it!" he exclaims.

"We did! What now?" Toño asks

Manuel's friend Armando is waiting for them at the bus station and takes them to the two-bedroom apartment in a run-down building in Brooklyn he found for them. The apartment is in the kind of neighborhood daughters aren't allowed to visit. Drug dealers linger on corners according to territorial lines neither Manuel nor Toño know exist. The two men learn to keep their heads down, go about their own business, and never speak to their neighbors.

Manuel taught Armando how to make gold chains when the two of them were in Los Angeles, before Toño arrived, and Armando returns the favor by introducing them to the local jeweler, an Indian man in a turban who, Armando says, always wears a tan suit. This is how, after a quick bus trip, Toño and Manuel are able to pick up their lives where they left them in Los Angeles, now in a new city.

Armando shows up on a Saturday night with a six-pack in hand. "Get dressed, there's a party tonight," he commands when he walks through the door.

Toño and Manuel have spent the day at the laundromat and are about to eat takeout Chinese for dinner. Empty Styrofoam containers from past meals have multiplied and litter the counters next to empty cans of beer and Coke.

"Where's the party?" Manuel asks through a mouthful of fried rice.

"Manhattan. My friend's kid is graduating or something like that. Should be plenty of women there." Armando opens the fridge and puts five of the six beers inside, keeping one for himself.

The three of them finish the beers while Toño and Manuel finish their meal and add their waste to the piles on the counter. Each man drinks an additional beer from Manuel's personal reserve before they get dressed and head out into the night. There is enough light from the city that never sleeps to see the trash littering the streets, but even if they couldn't see the garbage the smell would announce its presence.

The men pass by graffiti on the walls of the subway station and board the train. Three women find seats in the next car, the one behind theirs, and Armando tries to get their attention with a wave multiple times but none of them act like they notice. The women stay on the train when Toño and his friends get off at their stop.

"This way," Armando says outside the station. He turns to the left and walks ahead of Toño and Manuel until they get to an apartment building. After they are buzzed up, Armando leads the way up to the ninth floor.

Dozens of people are packed into a two-bedroom apartment. The addition of three more bodies doesn't register to the people farthest from the door. The room is dark, and there is a small area for dancing set up on one side of the living room. Armando recognizes his friend among the crowd and is able to squeeze his way forward by dancing through the mass of people. Toño and Manuel stay close behind, and Armando introduces them to his friend.

"Boys, I'd like you to meet Hector. Hector, meet my friends Manuel and Toño."

The men all shake hands.

"Where can a guy get a drink around here?" Armando asks.

Hector points to the kitchen next to the front door. The distance can't be more than twenty feet, but bodies are crammed into the space like fish caught in a net. The three men dance back to where they came from and discover the party is out of beer.

"Liquor or nothing, boys!" Armando says with a twinkle in his eye.

"Let's get this party started!" Manuel says.

Both men look at the third member of their group. "Toño?" Manuel says.

"Let's do it!" Toño replies.

Cranberry juice and vodka is the concoction of choice. The drink is poured strong, with just enough cranberry to color the mix. Toño's friends go back for their second, then their third, not realizing Toño still has his first drink in hand. Every time they make a new drink, Toño adds more cranberry juice to his glass, and by the time the taste becomes acceptable the party has died down, as if the weaker his drink gets the weaker the party becomes. His two friends spend their whole night trying to counteract the effect.

On Toño's last trip to add more cranberry juice to his cup, he comes face to face with a young woman with a bulge on her back. He has seen her around the party and decided she has a pretty face but couldn't make out her shape because she was sitting down near the dance floor. Now that she stands in front of him, Toño can see she is almost the archetype of a Central American woman: short, slender, dark-haired, and tan. Not unlike the sisters in his family, except for the added mass atop her shoulder blades.

Toño introduces himself and finds out her name is Paula. "Hector's younger sister," she adds. They are two of less than ten people left at the party, each of them sober counterparts to the people they accompany.

"Do you want some?" Toño asks, holding out the container of juice and shaking its contents.

Paula holds her breath and hesitates, thrown off by the clarity of the man in front of her. She is used to the drunk advances of men at these parties. "Sure," she says, the air in her lungs rushing out with the word. She holds up her cup and Toño begins to pour.

Toño points to his friends after filling her cup. "I came with those two," he says. Manuel and Armando have moved chairs into the middle of the dance floor and are deep in conversation with Hector and another man, despite the loud music right behind them.

"I saw," Paula says.

An ocean of silence descends between the two, the kind born when two people want to talk but have nothing to say.

"I can't believe the neighbors haven't said anything about the noise," Paula says, venturing into the unknown waters.

"I know!" says Toño. He clings to the conversation like it's a life preserver. "It's three in the morning. I thought we would have gone to a bar by now."

"And I thought I'd be on my way home."

"Where do you live?" Toño asks.

"Brooklyn. You?"

"Us too."

"You live with them?"

"No, I live with Manuel. Armando lives in Brooklyn too, a few blocks away."

Paula and Toño discover they live less than a ten-minute

walk away from each other. Toño can't help but hope he has found a woman he can spend some time with.

"Can I take you out?" he says.

"Sure. There's something you should know though," she says, her voice trailing off.

Toño lets the silence linger in the air while the possibilities of the silence run through his mind. Is she embarrassed of her hump? Does she have a kid?

"I'm married."

"Married?"

"To get my green card."

Toño takes a sip of his drink—very little vodka is left—and wishes it was stronger. He looks at Paula over the top of his cup.

"Don't look at me with those puppy eyes. There's nothing to be sad about! He comes around on the weekends," Paula explains. "During the week I live alone. You can take me out then."

None of what Paula said matters after he hears he can take her out. It's been so long since Toño has had the scent of a woman in his nostrils, he can't help but see red. "Tomorrow night?" he says.

"Sunday night?"

The tone of Paula's voice betrays her impatience. "I just said it has to be during the week!"

Hector notices how long his sister and Toño have been talking. Much longer than necessary, in his opinion. He calls out to his sister, "Paula! Make me another drink!"

"Same thing as last time?" she calls out over the music.

"Yes! I'm thirsty."

"One second," Paula says to Toño. She finds the whiskey and mixes one small shot with plenty of Coke. "Want to write down my number?" she asks Toño.

Toño searches through the drawers in Hector's kitchen and

finds pencil and paper. He writes down Paula's number and, once he finishes writing, asks if Tuesday will work.

Paula nods and walks to the dance floor. Toño notices how she stands upright even with the extra weight on her shoulders.

"Tuesday it is," he says to the bulge on her back.

CHAPTER SIXTEEN

Toño TAKES Paula on three dates before he is invited up to her apartment. Before she opens the door she tells Toño, "No funny business."

Toño raises his hands to profess his innocence.

Inside her apartment she tells Toño to take a seat on the couch. "I'll be right back. I want to show you something," she says before walking to her room.

Toño can't contain his excitement and fidgets in his seat.

Paula emerges from her room with just a bra on, two black-feathered wings emerging from her shoulders. One of them is crooked.

Toño's mouth hangs open and Paula tucks her wings behind her.

"What are you thinking?" she says, her voice as soft as her feathers.

Toño is pulled from his trance and mutters, "Are you an angel?"

Paula laughs. "No, no, I was born with these."

"Was the one always crooked like that?"

"My husband did that," she says. "It was an accident

though!"

Toño wonders why she defends this man if she is only with him for papers, but the sight of a woman in a bra dispels the thought from his mind.

Paula notices Toño staring at her chest and puts on an old oversized shirt.

"I told you, no funny business," she says.

"Of course not," Toño says.

Toño walks home through flurries, wishing he had brought a jacket and assuming the snowfall in June is another quirk of New York weather he has to get used to. Manuel is waiting up for him when he gets back.

"How was your night?" Manuel says, his white teeth in sharp contrast to the shadows around him.

"Dinner was good," Toño says as he takes a seat on the couch. He doesn't want to mention Paula's wings, at least not yet.

"Seeing you with her makes me miss Lenore," Manuel says, his eyes glued to the static on the television.

"Have you told her?"

"I did."

"And what did she say?"

"She'll be here tomorrow."

"Really! So she's the one?"

"I think so, Toño, I think so."

Toño looks around their apartment. He tries to see it with a woman's eyes and begins to notice the dishes in the sink and the trash from past meals on the counter. "We should clean up before she gets here," he says.

"That's also what I wanted to talk to you about. I'm moving out. There's a one-bedroom apartment in this building I've put my name on. This one will be all yours."

"I can't afford the rent by myself," Toño says.

"I took care of it. Dolores and Jorge are coming tomorrow too, they will take my room."

Toño is surprised his friend has been able to make all these arrangements behind his back. "When did you do all this?"

"A few weeks ago. I didn't do much, other than talk to Lenore. And find the one-bedroom. The rest of it was all her idea. Dolores said she wanted to surprise you."

"Well, I'm surprised."

Manuel and Toño take off work the next morning, clean up their place, and pick up the three travelers from the bus station.

"Hey baby," Manuel says to Lenore before he plants a kiss on her lips. This is the first time they have seen each other in months, and both are relieved their time apart has come to an end.

Toño shakes hands with Jorge before embracing Dolores. Jorge extends a hand to Manuel, but Manuel goes straight in for the hug.

"How was the trip?" asks Manuel, his arm around Lenore.

Dolores answers for the three of them. "Boring, very boring. This one slept most of the day!" she says as she hits Jorge on the shoulder with the back of her hand. "I've never seen anything like it. Even a crying baby on the second day couldn't keep him awake."

The group hails two cabs, and Manuel and Toño each get in one to direct the driver to their apartment. When they arrive, Manuel gives everyone the tour of the apartment where Toño will now live with Dolores and Jorge. He shows them the bathroom and points out where they can keep their toothbrushes, leads them into the room that is almost cleared for them, and makes the pair take in the view of the opposite building from the living room window. He even takes the time to point out the refrigerator and opens the appliance to display its contents: a few beers, leftover white rice, and two bottles of Coke.

"I think we can figure the rest out on our own," Jorge says, his voice cold, as if all the warmth of his patience was absorbed when the understocked refrigerator was opened.

Manuel leads the entire group to the new apartment where he will live with Lenore and repeats the same points of interest.

Toño, Manuel, and Jorge help move the rest of Manuel's belongings into his new apartment before Manuel and Toño sit down to finish the day's production.

Late at night, both men still hard at work, Manuel asks Toño if he's considered settling down with Paula.

"I'm still trying to spend the night with her!" Toño says with a laugh before he realizes his friend is serious. "We haven't talked about anything yet. I know she's getting her green card and plans to stay. Me, I'm saving money so I can go back to San Ramon and buy my farm. She can come with me."

"I can't believe you're still hung up on going back! You see the news, you know about the murders. The whole country is in a civil war! It isn't safe anymore."

"That's only in the capital. San Ramon is still safe," Toño says. It's true, at least according to his parents. Neither of them have mentioned any murders in their town during their phone conversations. All of his siblings are safe, and even if they weren't, it seems to Toño the place to be is by their side.

"The whole country is going to shit," Manuel says. "You should stay and be happy with Paula."

Toño doesn't respond and Manuel lets the matter drop. When they finish their work for the night, Manuel goes back to Lenore in his apartment, leaving Toño with the sense nothing will be quite the same anymore, their partnership has come to a close. Toño wonders if Beto felt the same way when he watched Toño leave for America and understands why someone would want to break another's wings, to keep them from flying away.

CHAPTER SEVENTEEN

THE MONTHS of summer arrive without the typical warm weather. On the hottest days the temperature approaches seventy degrees, but most days, with temperatures down in the fifties, require long pants and jackets. Toño and Paula develop a routine: she spends the night with Toño Monday and Wednesday nights each week. Sometimes Toño takes her out to dinner and sometimes Paula shows up, groceries in hand, and cooks them dinner. This is how Toño discovers Paula is able to control the utensils in the kitchen the same way his mother does: she sets the spoons stirring themselves and convinces the knife to chop for her. Paula makes enough food for Jorge and Dolores as well, and after Toño's roommates eat three meals in a row without reciprocating, Dolores offers to cook one Wednesday night in July

Paula arrives with just her overnight bag wearing a black dress, black sandals, and a black cardigan to cover her wings. Her curly hair is down and the faint smell of flowers follows her inside. When Toño informs her of Dolores's plan, a slight frenzy overtakes her and Toño doesn't understand why.

"Why didn't you tell me?" she says. "I would have brought

something!" This woman, married and leading a double life, has no reason to care what Dolores thinks about her etiquette.

"She just told me last night. I didn't think it would matter," Toño says.

"Of course it matters! She's your cousin!"

Dolores doesn't notice her guest showed up empty-handed, or if she does she doesn't act like it. For dinner she prepares slow-cooked chicken in self-stirred tomato sauce, white rice, salad tossed by an obedient bowl, and flan for dessert.

"So when did you come to the States?" Dolores asks Paula at the dinner table.

"Two years ago, to live with Hector."

"Two years ago you came to America? Or to New York?"

"Both. This is the first place I came. When did you come?"

"I crossed the border in 1979 and came to New York two months ago with Jorge," Dolores says.

"We came to America in the same month but didn't know about the other's plans," Toño says.

"Wow, what a coincidence! And Jorge, when did you come?"

"Manuel and I came over in '78."

"Did I meet Manuel at the party?" Paula asks Toño.

Toño nods, his mouth filled with food.

"Where did you come from?" Dolores asks.

"Honduras," Paula answers. "You all came from El Salvador, right?"

"From the same town," Dolores says. Jorge nods. "But I met Jorge here."

"And you're all illegal?" Paula says. She asks the question in an offhanded way, in order to advance the conversation, but Toño feels his stomach drop.

"We don't have papers, so yes. You?"

"I'm waiting to get my green card," she says. "But since I don't have it yet I'm illegal too," she adds with a smile.

Toño takes a drink of Coke and the coolness spreads relief to his stomach. His eyes meet Paula's and they exchange a smile. Two illegals in America. There is a rush from the thought they could be caught at any time, like they have their own secret the Americans are trying to discover. To say nothing about Paula's husband who, Paula assures Toño, doesn't suspect a thing.

"I've been trying to learn English," Paula says. "I try and learn from the shows I watch but it doesn't help. None of it makes sense!"

Toño tells Paula about Manuel and how his tongue was built to speak English. Jorge, when he hears the praise for his brother, pushes his plate away and announces he is finished eating.

Toño follows Jorge from the dinner table to the couch. They turn on the television and watch the news in silence. The women clean the dishes amidst constant chatter and Toño overhears Dolores give Paula tips about how to convince a rag to dry the dishes itself.

Jorge is the first man to utter a word since dinner. "Dolores, I'm going to bed." He stands up and goes into his room.

Dolores looks at the clock on the oven. "It's already eleven! The night has gotten away from us," she says with a smile towards Paula.

Paula takes a seat next to Toño on the couch. She runs her hand through his hair, then palms the back of his head. "We should probably get to bed too," she says, her voice soft and drowsy, the kind of voice Toño wants to lay his head on and rest after working week in and week out for months and years on end.

Dolores follows Jorge into their room.

While Toño sits with Paula, not paying attention to the

news, he wonders how he has been able to find a woman in this crowded city. Thoughts of marriage fill his mind and he wonders how she would look next to him on a farm in San Ramon. There's just one problem: she's already married. A wave of sadness hits Toño when he realizes the futility of their situation.

"Does your husband like your cooking?" Toño asks. He tries his best to hide the jealousy in his voice.

A dark veil descends over Paula's features. "He's never around," she says. She tells Toño how her husband, named Antonio too, prefers to go out for every meal during their weekends together.

"What does Hector think about all this?" Toño says in an effort to sound conversational.

"It all seems very natural to him. Antonio is my husband and he does what he has to in order to make money. Both of them act like it's only temporary, but I remember the green card is the only reason I got married in the first place."

Paula stands up and leads Toño into the room, which becomes theirs two nights a week.

Toño lies in bed confused. Paula's arrangement does seem normal and temporary, designed to allow the other Antonio time to make money for their future together. Not unlike his own situation, a temporary arrangement for his future in El Salvador. But Paula talks about her arrangement like it's just business, like her life after the green card isn't determined. Here she is, spending the night with another man, another Antonio, and the chemistry between them isn't imagined by either person. Her words don't match her actions, and to Toño, she seems like a woman who can't decide what she wants. As he drifts off to sleep he realizes he will have to decide for her.

CHAPTER EIGHTEEN

Toño DIVES into his assembly of gold chains with the sense that a future with Paula is his for the taking, a future dependent on him being able to provide. Fingers grasp little gold links while Toño makes plans to grasp his destiny and pull her close. On Friday he goes to the jeweler in Manhattan. The jeweler pays Toño for the week's production before giving him a bag of gold links half the size of the usual order.

"Is this everything?" Toño says, shaking the bag.

"There aren't many orders this week," the jeweler says. His eyes never stray from the ring he's inspecting.

"Do you know anyone who might have more orders?" he says.

The jeweler sets the ring down on the glass display case. "Are you threatening to work for someone else? If you are, you can give back the sack I just gave you."

Toño shakes his head no. "I need to make more money," he whispers, more to himself than to the man in front of him.

"Don't we all," the jeweler says, returning to the ring.

Toño looks past the jeweler's turban and sees his future slipping away in the display of gold necklaces, some of which he made.

When Toño doesn't move, the jeweler looks up again, ready for a fight. He pauses when he sees the sadness in Toño's eyes.

"I came to New York with just a backpack, ready to take on the world," the jeweler says.

Toño is pulled from his trance and looks at the man in front of him. The jeweler has deep lines around his eyes from a constant squint, and his cheeks sag from the weight of flesh added piecemeal over the years. "Me too," he says.

These are two immigrants, separated by time on their paths to stability.

"Tell you what," the jeweler says. "I split a full order into two and gave you half. Since you came here first I'll give you the full order and tell the other guy there isn't work this week," he says. He reaches under the counter and pulls out the other bag. "It's a little more than normal though," he adds.

"It'll be done by next week."

Toño gets a head start assembling the gold chains over the weekend and on Monday loses track of time while he works. Paula knocks on his door, a surprise before he realizes the time of day. They aren't able to leave for dinner without Toño asking Paula when she's leaving her husband.

"I tried to bring it up to him this weekend and I couldn't do it," Paula says. "I'm scared I won't be able to get my green card."

"You need to tell him about us," Toño says.

Paula looks at Toño with tear-filled eyes. Her wings press against the coat on her back and she unzips the front to give the appendages more space. "And what if I don't?"

No words come from Toño. He looks at her while trying to decide if he was wrong about her ability to leave her husband for him.

Paula can't handle the silence. "Don't look at me with those sad eyes! I don't know if I can tell him. It isn't an easy topic to bring up."

"If you don't tell him, we will have to stop seeing each other," Toño says.

Tears begin to fall from Paula's eyes, streak down her cheek, and fall onto her shirt.

"Why can't you just enjoy what we have?" she pleads.

"Because I want more. I want to get married, have kids."

"But I don't want what you want! Why are you even wasting your time with a married woman if you can't handle it? Do you know how many women are in this city, Toño?"

"I don't and I don't care." Toño's stomach rumbles, shaking the cans on the counter. "Let's go eat," he says.

They go to a Salvadoran restaurant near Toño's apartment, both wearing winter clothes even though it's the middle of summer. Their entire meal is spent in silence. On the walk back Toño tells Paula his ultimate goal: for them to marry, move back to San Ramon, and live on a farm of their own.

"Land everywhere! Fresh air. Privacy," Toño says once they are seated on the couch, fajitas digesting in their stomachs.

Paula turns up her nose. "But there's nothing to do on a farm. It can get lonely."

"You want to live closer to San Salvador?"

"Why are you so intent on going back at all? You came here for a reason. Don't you like it here?"

Toño pauses and his gaze falls to the floor. "I came here to make money because I hate being poor," he says, his voice cracking. The word "hate" drips from his tongue like poison.

Paula wraps her arms around him. "There's plenty of money to be made in the States," she says while she rubs his shoulder.

"You want to stay here?"

Paula pulls her arms away and crosses her hands in her lap. "It doesn't matter what I want."

"It does to me. Why are you so against going back?"

Paula exhales. "Nobody notices me in the city," she says. "They don't notice the bulge on my back, and if they do, they don't ask any questions."

Toño wraps a hand around her shoulder, her feathers tickling his elbow.

"There isn't anybody on a farm," he says.

"But people in town talk! Why do you think I wanted to come to America in the first place? Everyone knew about my wings. And they talked!" Paula suppresses a sob. "There were so many rumors, I stopped leaving the house. My mother calls them my angel wings, but angels don't have black wings."

"You made a deal with the devil," Toño says to himself, remembering what his sisters said about Hortensia, about her red nails and lips.

Paula recoils and sits on the far side of the couch. She stares at Toño with a fire in her eyes he has never seen before.

"My sisters used to say the same thing about a girl in my town," Toño says in an effort to explain himself. "I wasn't saying you did."

"That's what everyone used to say," she says. Her wings weigh down her shoulders and her chin follows. "Here, even if I did make a deal with the devil, no one cares!"

"And you want your papers so you can stay here. When will they be finished?"

"I don't know, Toño, these things take time."

Toño moves across the couch and rests his hand on Paula's leg. She pulls it off. He gets up and turns the volume up on the television before sitting back down. They are both grateful for the added noise, and the evening passes by without another mention of the future.

In bed that night, Paula slides in close to Toño. Most nights this movement is enough to prompt her companion into action, but tonight he turns his back to her and continues to sleep, hoping he will wake up and not remember the woman with wings.

CHAPTER NINETEEN

SUMMER HEAT still hasn't arrived when Manuel tells Toño about Lenore's pregnancy. The two friends see little of each other over the following months as Manuel stays busy preparing for his daughter's arrival. In spring of the following year, the phone rings, and Toño, Dolores, and Jorge all go to Manuel's apartment to see the new baby.

Toño can tell Manuel has changed at first glance. His friend has always been a happy man—whether his teeth grew because of his happiness or his happiness grew because of his teeth, nobody knows—but now another emotion is present. It could be pride, it could be purpose, but whatever it is, Manuel seems to have crossed a chasm and left his Toño along on the far side.

The baby is bundled in blankets and Lenore refuses to let anyone else hold her, an attitude Toño is grateful for because he has no desire to hold the tiny human.

The weather still hasn't warmed up in June when Manuel invites Toño to go for a walk in Central Park with him and his daughter, now two months old. Toño arrives at his friend's apartment at eight on a Sunday morning, and from the bags under Manuel's eyes, he gets the sense his friend hasn't been able to give attention to anything other than the baby.

"She doesn't like to sleep," he says as he shuts the door behind Toño. "I've already been awake for hours."

Toño walks right over to the baby on the couch and looks down at her. She has on tiny white shorts, a tiny blue shirt, and no shoes. Her hair, jet black, is matted against her head. Her eyes are closed.

"She's asleep now," Toño says.

"It will only last for a few minutes. Half an hour if I'm lucky. Not long enough for me to lay down and sleep."

"Where's Lenore?"

Manuel points to the room behind him. "I let her sleep. She has to wake up and feed the baby so often that once morning comes she's exhausted."

"You look exhausted too."

"That's because I am."

Manuel prepares his daughter to travel, complete with coat, hat, and tiny gloves, and the three of them take the subway into Manhattan. The sunlight outside the station blinds the two men, but the trees in Central Park reach up to get as close as they can to the source. It appears that all of New York is able to ignore the cold June weather, because the lawns are covered with picnickers and runners litter the paved footpaths. Manuel pushes the stroller and the three of them descend into the shade thrown down by the bright green leaves overhead.

"Are you still seeing that woman?" Manuel asks.

"Paula? Yes."

"Married, isn't she?"

"For papers."

"Does it take this long for papers?"

"Don't know, I don't have mine."

Manuel sighs. "Don't you ever miss going out to meet new people, new women?"

"No, too much work to do," Toño says. He doesn't mention how he never liked these things to begin with.

"What do you do on the weekends? We haven't seen much of each other for months now."

"Same things I did when we lived together: laundry, eat, sleep. Sometimes I'll walk around the city."

"With your woman?"

"No, she's with her husband on the weekends."

Manuel shakes his head.

"She keeps saying she will leave him after she gets her papers," Toño says in an effort to explain himself.

"Will she though? She seems content to keep you where you are."

Toño watches a bird fly overhead. "It's complicated."

The friends walk in silence, each lost in their own thoughts, as a breeze ruffles the leaves of the trees.

"I got a new job," Manuel says.

"You did? No more gold chains?"

"I've only been doing that here and there for some extra cash. I was translating for an acting studio and they asked me to be there full time. Steady income but now I have to go to work every day instead of sitting at home, watching what I want on TV. But I get to practice my English!"

"Good, the jeweler tried to give me less work this week. You don't need that headache."

"I've got my hands full already!"

"How many do you want to have?" Toño says with a nod to the baby inside the stroller.

"Beats me. I know Lenore wants more but who knows how many."

"You should have three," Toño says.

"Three? Why three?"

"Well, you can't have just one. With one there is nothing to compare."

Manuel and Toño take a seat on a wooden bench alongside the path and watch a group of runners pass by.

Toño continues, "You don't know if it's smart, dumb, or sick. It could have problems in school . . . you just don't know. With two you have a better chance of a successful one. So you can compare."

Manuel laughs, his white teeth on full display. "How much thought have you given this?"

Toño smiles and continues his stream of thoughts, ignoring his friend's question.

"Everyone wants to have a boy and a girl but that doesn't matter. What matters is that you can see how the other one is and adjust."

"Okay, that makes sense. But why three?"

Toño's sad eyes twinkle with the masterstroke of his advice on the tip of his tongue. "The third is for you. With three, two of them can be together and leave you out of their plans. The third one can tell you what's going on. That way, you and Lenore can know what your kids are up to. You can work the friendships. Plus, it's another chance for you to compare."

"When did you think about all this?"

Toño shrugs. "It's just the way I think," he says. He had no awareness of this position before it was spoken, but the logic seems so obvious to him no thought is required. Like the color blue. There is never a conscious thought associated with blue; it just exists, and so do his reasons for three children. If he was still in El Salvador, his mother would have been able to tell him that when this is the case, it's because his memory is working in reverse.

The two friends get up from the bench and continue on

their walk. Manuel keeps one eye on his daughter to see if anything catches her eye even though she is too young to appreciate her surroundings.

After the friends get lunch at McDonald's, Toño's restaurant of choice, they board the subway back to Brooklyn. Toño brings up the most recent news out of El Salvador. "My father said the killings are getting worse."

Manuel leans forward and puts his pinky finger into his daughter's tiny hand. "I saw on the news," he says, shaking his head. "Only you could talk about death with a baby right in front of your face."

"He said the guerrillas used to kill in secret then run away, worried they would get caught. Now they walk right up to the target in broad daylight and pow!" Toño slams a fist into his palm. "He said there was a murder in the market last week."

Manuel has no interest in the violence of the town. His mother lives in the capital and her safety is his only concern in their home country. Even so, his curiosity gets the best of him. "Gunshot?" Manuel asks. His daughter's fingers wrap around his finger.

"Yes, right near the fountain. The priest was nearby and gave the man his last rites." The train stops and more passengers board than disembark.

"I need to start going to mass again," Manuel says when the train begins to move again.

"Why?"

"So I can teach her. One day you will have to worry about these things too!"

"When I have a family of my own," Toño says, with a dash of longing in his voice.

"You could have one if you weren't so stubborn."

Toño assumes Manuel is talking about Paula. "I'm not the

stubborn one, she is. She's the one who won't leave her husband."

"Because she wants to stay here! You could get your green card too, I'm sure it would change things."

"She shouldn't care about a piece of paper," Toño says.

Manuel pulls his finger away from his daughter. "Would you stay for her?"

Toño is saved from responding by the doors of the train opening at their stop. The two men get off, walk back to their building, and go to their separate apartments. As Toño closes the door he says "yes" to his living room, sure that wings on a woman might as well be a target and unsure if the priest would bother to stop.

CHAPTER TWENTY

BENITO, a friend from Toño's hometown, calls Toño on a Thursday night at the end of summer.

"Your mother gave me your number," he explains. "She said you were in New York. I'm in Maryland!"

"Just down the coast," Toño says, unsure of the distance.

Benito informs Toño that his wedding will be next Saturday and he would love for his former neighbor to be there. The two men talk for another hour about the time since they last saw each other, each of them relaying the story of their border crossing and the paths they took to their current locations. Toño mentions his trip across the country with Manuel, and Benito extends the invitation to him as well.

"He has a woman now, Lenore, and they have a baby. He's busy all the time, but I'll tell him, maybe he can come," Toño says.

"Tell him, you never know."

Toño gets off the phone and calls Paula to see if she would like to come with him, forgetting her standing conflict on weekends. The phone is picked up on the third ring.

"Hello?" Paula says.

"It's me, Toño."

"Sorry, I think you have the wrong number."

"Paula, I know it's you. I have a question for you."

"No problem! Have a good day," Paula says before she hangs up.

Toño stares at the receiver in his hand, his stomach in knots from knowing the other Antonio is there. Toño decides right then and there to avoid Paula until he gets back from his trip.

On Friday, before he goes to the jeweler, Toño goes to the Greyhound depot in Manhattan and buys a ticket to Washington, D.C. With next week's order of gold chains in hand, he stops by his favorite Blimpie for a sandwich before riding the train back to Brooklyn. When he calls Benito, telling him when and where the bus will drop him off, his friend tells him he will make arrangements to have him picked up at the station.

Toño accompanies Manuel and his family to church on Sunday and mentions his upcoming trip to Maryland on their way home from lunch.

"Why didn't you invite me?" Manuel says. Lenore walks behind them, pushing the baby in her stroller.

"He told me to invite you, but I didn't think you could go."

"And why not?" Manuel demands. Toño has known his friend long enough to know this display of anger is a front.

"Because of the baby! She's still so small."

"But she's growing like a weed!" Manuel says. "Who knows, by next week she could double in size." Manuel looks down into the stroller and is smiling when he turns his attention back to Toño, his teeth on full display. "You're right though, that's a long trip for a baby."

"Should we send a present?" Manuel asks Lenore.

"Could be a good idea. Something small," she says.

"Okay, get them something and Toño will take it with him."

The following Friday morning, before he leaves, Toño picks

up a small box wrapped in white paper from Lenore while Manuel is at work. "It's a picture frame," Lenore says.

Instead of forcing the gift into his stuffed backpack, Toño holds the white box on his way to the station and onto the bus, and still has the gift in hand when the bus stops in Washington, D.C., late Friday night. The bus depot itself looks the same as the one he left in New York, but there's a distinct difference in the skyline. In New York all he had to do was look around and a skyscraper could be seen in the distance. This isn't the case in the nation's capital. He looks at the buildings around him, dwarves compared to what he is used to in New York, and in the distance the Washington Monument rises above all else, stark white against the night sky.

As Toño waits to get off the bus, his attention is drawn to a short, squat man with the face of a bear, complete with fur, on the sidewalk. The man approaches every hispanic-looking male who gets off the bus before Toño. When Toño gets to the top of the stairs he hears his name.

"Toño?" the bear says to one man who gets off the bus two people ahead of Toño. The man the question is directed to is tan, and it's clear, to Toño at least, he is from India or somewhere else in that part of the world. He could even be related to the New York jeweler, although he doesn't wear a turban. Toño laughs to himself before he thanks the driver for the ride and walks down the steps.

"Toño?"

"That's me. Did Benito ask you to pick me up?" Toño says. He extends his hand and the bear grabs it, relief spreading across his face.

"He did. I'm his friend Esteban. Do you have any luggage?" the bear asks with a nod towards the undercarriage of the bus.

Toño taps one of the straps hanging from his shoulders. "No, everything I need is in here."

"Great! I parked over there." Esteban leads Toño to a champagne-colored sedan parked near the back of the lot. The two men get in and drive an hour north into Maryland to the apartment where Benito lives.

Benito gives Toño a hug when he sees his old friend. He has put on weight since the last time Toño saw him. His heavy cheeks are in a fight against gravity, and his belt strains to keep the button on his pants from popping off. The man has held onto the belief that he is a particular waist size for far too long; his belly hangs over the buckle.

The bear helps himself to a beer from the refrigerator. Toño is surprised at how at home this man makes himself, but Benito doesn't give the man a second thought. Benito offers a beer to Toño, who accepts, and yells for the bear to grab a beer for each of them as well. Toño throws his backpack onto the couch and gives Manuel's gift to Benito, who puts it on the end table, before the three men sit down at the kitchen table.

Benito asks Toño how life in New York is treating him. Toño confides in his friend how the jeweler tried to give him less work and his worry about what will happen if the work slows down.

"There's money to be made here in Maryland," Benito says. "It's not the same kind of work you do now, I don't know of anyone who makes gold chains, but there are always restaurants looking for dishwashers."

"I've never worked as a dishwasher before," Toño says.

"It's easy and it never ends. Not like your gold chains." Benito pauses. "You should move down here! It would be nice to have an old friend around."

"It could be time for another adventure," Toño says.

After Esteban leaves and Benito goes to bed, Toño lays on the couch wondering what Paula would say about a move to Maryland before he falls asleep.

The next day, the day of the wedding, Esteban the bear takes Toño with him to drop off the alcohol for the reception before they head to the church. They load three coolers of beer and two boxes of liquor into the bed of a pickup truck Esteban has parked out front. Less than ten minutes into their drive, Esteban points out the church where the service will be held, and five minutes later they park next to an outdoor pavilion at a local park.

Four women are putting the finishing touches on the decorations. Streamers hang from the sides of the roof and snake their way down all eight pillars. White plastic tablecloths, taped down to prevent them from blowing away, cover the six wooden tables. Two of the women, the younger two, wear sundresses and high heels. The older two look like they could be Toño's grandmother and wear aprons over their clothes and flat, well-worn sandals. The aproned women are grilling meat for the party, and judging from their outfits, won't be going to church. Esteban and Toño ask where the beer should be placed and are pointed to one end of a table covered with aluminum trays. Each tray, waiting to be filled with food, has a burner underneath.

"We need to get going," one of the younger women says.

"I'm almost done," the other well-dressed woman replies. She tapes down the final streamer before the two of them step back to admire their handiwork.

The younger women walk up to the older women and Toño hears them say they will see them soon, the food smells delicious, and they are grateful the two women were able to help today.

The bear looks at Toño with a twinkle in his eye. "Let's have a beer before we head over."

They sit down at a picnic table, a playground full of children in the distance. "How long until Benito has one of his own?" Esteban says.

"Until he has a beer? As soon as he gets here I would think."

"No, not a beer! A kid."

Toño laughs. "Bet it will be quick. Why else would they get married?"

"You haven't met Isabel."

When their beers are finished, they leave the women alone in the park and are the last two to arrive at church. Esteban rushes to the front of the room to stand among the men at Benito's side, and Toño sits down as the priest makes his way to the pulpit.

When the service is over, everyone makes their way to the pavilion for the reception. Speakers have been set up by the DJ while they were at church, and now Spanish music rings out over the summer air. The meat has all been grilled, and the two older women have filled the aluminum trays with meat, rice, green beans, and pasta.

A black limo with white streamers pouring from the windows pulls into the parking lot. The guests all cheer when the newlyweds step out, and in response, Benito lifts his wife's hand high in the air as if she just won a fight. Isabel beams with pride.

This is the first time Toño has seen Benito's bride. Her nose and chin come to a point, her cheekbones are high and pointed, and her smile exposes a mouthful of white teeth, each one razor sharp. She is thin and bony, and her elbows would have cut through the sleeves of her dress if she hadn't chosen a sleeveless variety for the occasion. All of her features blend together to produce a beauty in a way that leaves the impression she is not to be trifled with. Benito, with his easygoing personality, will have his fleshy hands full.

Toño manages to stay out of every picture: the moment the

couple first arrives, their first dance, the cutting of the cake, and the rest of the activities the couple participates in over the course of the evening. The reception ends when the alcohol runs out, well after the sun has gone down. Everyone in attendance leaves with full stomachs, throbbing hearts, and the memory of the best night they've ever had.

Esteban takes Toño to the bus depot the next morning with sunglasses on, still reeking of alcohol.

Toño suspects the man might still be drunk. He wanted to say goodbye to Benito but didn't dare disturb the sleeping couple in case Isabel chose to unleash a tongue as sharp as her features. Toño remembers the rattlesnake he encountered when he crossed the border and is thankful his friend got bitten instead of him.

CHAPTER TWENTY-ONE

THE THOUGHT of moving to Maryland haunts Toño from the moment he walks off the bus in New York and is disgusted by the smell of the city he calls home.

When Toño gets back from picking up the week's gold links, Paula calls and tells him they won't be able to see each other tonight. Hector, her brother, has made plans for his new girl-friend to come over for dinner, and Paula wants to cook for them. She could get out of the dinner but, as she explains to Toño, Hector has been secretive about his relationship until now. Paula feels a corner has been turned and Hector wants this new woman to be a part of the family.

Toño accepts the cancelation without a second thought. His gut tells him she still hasn't talked to her husband about her weekday relationship, and the last thing he wants to deal with is more tears when he brings the topic up yet again.

While Toño's fingers assemble gold chains Monday night, Tuesday, and Wednesday morning, all Toño can think about is moving to Maryland. He decides he must tell Paula she can either agree to come with him or he will leave her. He doesn't want to deal with the tears in person so he picks up the phone, only to hear Dolores already on the line, talking on the phone in her bedroom.

"Sorry," Toño says, hanging up.

He wants to keep up the momentum of his decision, so he looks out his window to the phone booth in front of his building, makes sure it's not in use, and grabs quarters before he walks outside.

"Hello?" Paula says.

"It's me, Toño."

"Hi, Toño!"

"Look, I have to tell you something."

Toño gives Paula the ultimatum and floats an inch above the ground without the weight on his shoulders.

Paula doesn't say a word for what seems like an hour. "What's in Maryland?" Her voice is weak and Toño has trouble hearing her.

"Work." He pauses, waiting to see if Paula will say anything. "Look, if you don't tell your husband you're leaving him I'm gone."

When Paula speaks again she tells Toño she was going to wait for tonight to tell him her news.

"You know how I have a broken wing, right?"

"Yes."

"He broke my other one over the weekend."

The walls of the phone booth contract around Toño, coming to a point opposite the sliding door. "If you had left him for me this wouldn't have happened."

"But it did happen."

"What do you want me to do?"

"I don't know! Listen, act like you care."

"Move to Maryland with me."

"I can't."

The phone booth's door slides open and Toño realizes this is the end. "Then what was the point in telling me about your broken wing? It's not my job to save you when you won't make a simple decision."

Paula begins to cry. "How could you leave me like this?" she says, her voice distorted with emotion.

"Leave you?" Toño yells. "It's better than what you did to me, keeping me around during the week so you have something, someone, to do!" Toño exhales while Paula sobs on the other end of the line. Her tears pass through the phone lines and drip from Toño's mouthpiece. "Is your mind made up?" Toño asks.

"I don't have a choice."

"You do!"

"I don't! I can't go with you, Toño. I'm sorry."

Toño slams the phone onto the receiver and the phone booth returns to its original shape.

Dolores is in the living room when Toño gets back to the apartment. "My mother says to tell you hi," she says.

Toño grabs an apple from a pile on the counter and twists the fruit to remove the stem. "How's she doing?"

"As well as she can with a civil war tearing the country apart."

Toño takes a monstrous first bite of his apple, a full half of the fruit, and nods. "I'm moving to Maryland," Toño says when enough of the fruit has been chewed for him to talk.

"Is that so?" Dolores replies. "You enjoyed your trip that much?"

"Benito said there's work for me."

"And what are we supposed to do for your part of the rent?"

Toño's teeth have pierced the skin of the apple before he stops and pulls the fruit away from his mouth.

"I've paid through this month."

"But the lease is under your name," Dolores says. She can tell Toño hasn't considered this.

"Then we can either transfer it to you or the two of you can move out."

Dolores raises her eyebrows, and Toño takes the interrupted bite.

"We were going to ask you about getting on the lease anyways," Dolores says. "We need an address to get our green cards."

"I'll talk to the landlord tomorrow. You guys decided to stay here?"

"El Salvador is in a civil war, only a fool would go back."

"I plan on going back."

"Then you're a fool!" Dolores says with a laugh. "When are you leaving?"

"Friday."

"Did you tell Paula?"

"I did. She won't come with me." Toño takes a series of small bites of his apple, clearing every bit of skin except from the top and bottom.

Dolores's face drops with sadness for her cousin and sadness for the woman who has become her friend. "It isn't easy for her, caught between you two."

"So I'm making her life easier by leaving."

"Are you taking everything with you?" she asks.

"No, I'll leave my bed and dresser here."

"You already got your ticket?"

"Not yet, I'm getting it tomorrow. Can you come with me to the landlord's tomorrow morning so we can transfer the lease to you?"

"Tomorrow morning? Works for me."

"Perfect," Toño says. "Let me call Benito and tell him I'm coming this weekend."

"Benito doesn't even know?" Dolores laughs and shakes her head. "Only you, Toño."

"He's the one who told me to move down! I just have to tell him it's this weekend."

"People don't like surprises, Toño," Dolores says.

"Let me call him now."

Benito tries to convince Toño not to come without ever saying so. He claims his wife needs more time to get the house clean, but Toño insists he doesn't mind the mess. He tries to say there won't be anyone to pick him up, but Toño says he'll get a cab. Toño disarms every reason Benito offers for why his friend shouldn't come and hangs up the phone after eating the last bit of flesh from his apple.

PART 3

FEAST OR FAMINE

CHAPTER TWENTY-TWO

Toño's BUS pulls into the D.C. depot just before eight at night. Both Benito and Esteban the bear wait for him on the sidewalk.

"Did you have to wait long?" Toño asks after the men say hello again for the second time in less than a week.

"Not long, we just got here," says Benito.

Esteban nods in agreement.

"Good. The bus got here right on time!" Toño says. He adjusts his backpack and waits for the two men to lead the way back to their car.

"Don't you have to get your luggage?" Benito says, pointing to the undercarriage of the bus.

Toño points over his shoulder with his thumb. "This is everything!"

"Really?" the bear says with wide eyes. He glances at Benito with a look that says, "This guy is crazy!"

Benito responds to the bear's look with a shrug before he turns around and walks towards the parking lot.

The city, so different from New York, provides Toño with the sense of home he hasn't felt since he was back in El Salvador. No disagreeable odors find his nostrils, and there is more greenery on the walk from the bus to the parking lot than anywhere in New York outside of Central Park.

Toño watches the Washington Monument tower over the city from the back seat of Benito's car. Benito turns the heat to max, claiming he's cold, even though the temperature outside is well above ninety. Toño's imposition after years without contact has caused Benito's temperature to drop, and the other two men have to suffer through the heat. Toño doesn't mind, but Esteban's fur sticks to his face in lines from where the sweat falls from his forehead.

Toño watches the Potomac River pass by. "Is there a beach around here?" Toño asks. The randomness of his question surprises the two men.

"It's a few hours away. I haven't been there before but Esteban has. Do you like it?" Benito says, deferring to his passenger.

"It's nice out there," Esteban says, his words punctuated by heavy breathing. The heat makes it hard for him to breathe. "Plenty of stuff to do on the boardwalk, lots of shops."

"We should go sometime! Maybe one weekend before it gets cold," Toño says. He leans forward and pats Benito on the shoulder. "The sun will warm you up!"

"Maybe," Benito says. He looks back before changing lanes.

"It all depends on Isabel," Esteban says.

"No it doesn't," Benito says.

Esteban ignores Benito. "If she wants to go then he'll go. If she doesn't then he stays home. Simple as that!"

Toño laughs as Benito's face gets red. Without warning, Benito leans forward and turns off the heat then demands everyone roll down their windows. "It got too hot," he explains.

"He doesn't do anything without her," Esteban says.

Toño flashes Benito a wide smile through the rearview mirror. Benito laughs, shakes his head, then admits it's true.

Benito parks the car outside his apartment in Gaithersburg, Maryland, and Toño follows the two men inside.

"Toño! It's so good to see you again," Isabel says when the three men enter the kitchen. The greeting sounds fake, staged in order to keep up appearances.

Toño suffers through a bony embrace, wondering how long her act will continue. Three wooden spoons stir the contents of three metal pots on the stove behind her; the smell of boiled chicken and onions fills the air. The broom stands at attention in the corner, awaiting instructions, reminding Toño of his mother's command of her own kitchen. Isabel shows her skill in a way Toño has never seen before: the sponge in the sink makes slow, clockwise circles over a dirty pan as steaming water runs from the tap. Without running water in El Salvador, Felicita would never trust a sponge to do the work when she could get it done much faster on her own and conserve water in the process.

"Benito said you'll be staying here?" she says, returning to her cooking after they part.

Her question takes Toño by surprise. He expected any business about living arrangements to be addressed by his friend. "Yes, he invited me before the wedding."

"Oh, he did? How nice of him!" Isabel says. She casts a disapproving look at her husband.

Benito lowers his head.

Esteban rummages through the refrigerator and pulls out a beer.

The woman of the house continues. "Do you know how long you'll be staying?"

"No idea," Toño says. He finds more words when he sees the momentary contraction of Isabel's features, like she just sucked a lemon. "Not long, I hope. Once I find work and get myself situated I'll be gone." Toño looks at Benito, his eyes searching. Why is he letting her ask these questions?

"Well, you keep us posted. If you need help with anything you just let us know. We're here for you."

Toño doesn't appreciate the way she emphasizes "you," but her sharp smile scrubs away the speculation of what she could have meant from his mind.

"Toño, you want a beer?" Esteban asks.

"I'll take one, sure."

"'Nito?"

"Not now, I'm going to bed soon."

The three men sit at the kitchen table and talk while Isabel finishes tomorrow's meal. When the food is finished, she pours the contents of the pot into three large containers and leaves them out to cool. She places the pots into the sink and the sponge begins its work. "Can you put these in the refrigerator before you go to sleep?" she tells Toño, pointing to the containers.

Toño nods his head, and Isabel walks out of the kitchen. A moment later her bedroom door clicks shut.

"Make sure you lock the door on your way out," Benito tells Esteban. He wishes both men good night and leaves them alone in the kitchen. A few minutes later, a heated discussion can be heard from the bedroom. Toño tries to eavesdrop, but Esteban finds reasons to keep talking.

"So, what's your plan?"

"Benito said there's work. So I guess I'll find a job."

"There's plenty of work as long as you don't mind shitty jobs," Esteban says with a snarl.

"What do you do?"

"Landscaping."

Toño turns his nose up at the thought of working outside.

Esteban laughs. "It's not for everyone. Benito said you could stay here?"

"Well, he told me to come down. Where else would I stay?"

Esteban finishes his beer with one long swig. "Good point. Come Monday we will have to find you a job." He stands up, sets the bottle on the counter, and pats Toño on the shoulder, telling him they will see each other tomorrow.

Toño finishes his beer alone in the kitchen and places his empty bottle next to Esteban's. He puts the food, still warm to the touch, away and decides to help the sponge by cleaning the dirty pots in the sink.

The broom catches Toño's eye before he turns off the kitchen lights. A command to sweep the floor causes the broom to rattle, but it doesn't move from its spot in the corner. Once his fingers are wrapped around the handle he can feel the broom come to life, and he directs it to sweep the floor, even though there's nothing to sweep—the broom in one outstretched arm, in order to convince himself he's still got it.

CHAPTER TWENTY-THREE

THE SECOND DAY of Toño's job search takes him to a large hotel on Frederick Road. He isn't sure what kind of job he can do with his limited English, but he figures he might as well ask. The smell of chlorine hits him when he walks through the sliding automatic doors, and he can see sunlight reflect off the pool's surface through another door on the opposite end of the building. The patterned green carpet creates an unsettling contrast with the light wood paneling on the walls in the dim light cast by sparse overhead lighting. A short Caucasian woman smiles at him from the front desk.

"How can I help you?" she says.

"I'm looking for a job," Toño replies in English. The words make his tongue feel too big for his mouth.

"Let me get my manager. Take a seat," she says, directing him to the padded chairs in the lounge.

He doesn't wait long before an African man walks over and introduces himself. "Philip," the man says with a hint of a French accent.

"Antonio."

"Claire tells me you're looking for a job. Have you ever worked in a hotel before?"

Toño shakes his head no.

"Let me think." Philip looks around the hotel and his eyes settle on the banquet hall. "You're young. Would you be interested in moving tables?"

"Sure," Toño says.

"We have a banquet this Friday night. Could you be here to help set up? If that goes well, we can discuss hiring you full time."

Toño hasn't heard of a banquet before, but he knows he can move tables, so he agrees to be there Friday night.

Philip looks at Toño's clothes: faded jeans and a threadbare T-shirt. "You'll need a uniform. What size are you?"

"Medium," Toño says.

"No, measurements."

Toño doesn't understand. "Not sure," he says.

"Hold on," says Philip. He goes to the front desk and asks Claire to find him a tape measure. She rummages through numerous drawers before she finds one. The man measures Toño's neck, arms, and legs.

"Be here Friday at four. And bring black dress shoes," Philip says. He waits for Toño to nod his understanding before walking away.

Isabel is ecstatic when she hears Toño has found a job. "How much will they pay you?" she asks. The two of them and Benito are seated around the table while they eat dinner: chicken soup and tortillas.

"Not sure."

"When do you start?" asks Benito.

Toño takes a large bite of chicken. "Friday. This soup is good!" he manages to say with a full mouth.

"Friday? What are you supposed to do until then?" says Isabel.

Benito reaches for another tortilla, his third. "Does it matter? Congratulations on finding work, Toño! This is exciting! I told you there's plenty of work here."

Isabel shoots her husband an icy glare. "I don't want him laying around all day the same way Esteban did when he first got here."

"He already has a job and he's only been here for a few days. Relax." Benito averts his wife's gaze and brings another spoonful of soup to his mouth, only to find the soup has frozen solid.

The corners of Isabel's mouth turn up in a sneer.

Benito pries the block of soup from the spoon with his teeth and smiles back, not wanting to let his wife know her decision to turn down the temperature has affected him in any way.

"What will you do until Friday?" Isabel asks again.

Toño wants to tell her he will relax, take it easy, and enjoy his time off, even though this would be a lie, just to see her reaction. He wants to work more than Isabel wants him to work; each day without a job is a wasted chance to earn money. "I'll try and find another job in case this one doesn't work out," he says.

Isabel leans back in her chair, satisfied with her houseguest's answer. "Good," she says before she tears a piece of tortilla off from the whole and places it on her sharp tongue.

Toño brings a steaming spoonful of soup to his mouth without waiting for it to cool down.

On Wednesday and Thursday, in order to placate Isabel, Toño leaves the house early and comes home late. "No luck," he tells the couple each night at dinner.

"The hotel will work out," Benito says both nights.

"Try harder," Isabel says with her eyes.

The walk to the hotel on Friday takes Toño forty-five minutes, a fact he notices in case he gets the job, and he arrives a full hour early, with Benito's black dress shoes on his feet.

Philip spots Toño right away. He puts his arm around Toño and leads him through an empty banquet hall, one of three, to the attached kitchen behind. "This is where they'll make the food. It will be your job to carry it out to the tables," Philip says.

Toño hangs onto every word, careful to translate each one in his mind so he doesn't miss any other duties required by his new position. Philip, continuing the tour, takes Toño into a hallway that runs perpendicular to the three banquet halls. Off of this hallway, next to the kitchen, is a large room filled with folded tables and chairs organized into neat rows.

"This is where I need your help the most," Philip says. "A young guy like you should have no problem setting these up. Your job will be to help William, the manager. You'll meet him soon. He will tell you how to arrange everything. Just listen to him and you'll be all right."

The last stop of the tour is an office behind the front desk. Claire must have the day off because a young man, about the same age as Toño, is the clerk today. Philip ignores him and leads Toño into the office. A dry cleaner's bag hangs from the coat rack.

"This is your uniform. Here, try it on," Philip says. He hands Toño black pants, a black vest, a white shirt, and a black bow tie.

The uniform is a perfect fit. Once this is confirmed, Philip tells Toño to change back into his other clothes so he can move furniture without getting the new uniform dusty or sweaty.

"William won't be here for another half hour so just hang out for now. Once he gets here the two of you can get started. He'll tell you what to do."

Toño explores the hotel while he waits for the manager to

arrive. He is drawn to the pool outside and checks to see if there are any good-looking women getting some sun. He is disappointed to find three older ladies, one old man, seven children, and two pairs of parents at the pool, not one of them worth looking at. Not one of them pays Toño any attention.

A shadow is cast over Toño while he wonders if he's turned into a ghost. "Antonio?" the shadow says.

Toño turns to the man next to him, squints his eyes, and positions his head so the man's body will block out the sun. "That's me," he says.

The man extends his hand. "William," he says. An older white man, he wears jeans and a button-down with the sleeves rolled up to his elbows. His eyes haven't had the pleasure of a good night's sleep in years, his teeth are stained yellow from cigarettes, and the smell of tobacco emanates from his pores. Nobody notices this man either.

"Let's go, lots to do," William says, leading Toño back inside. They end up in the room with the tables and chairs. The manager stretches his arms out wide in front of the tables, which stand vertically in a row. "We need to get all of these," he says in slow, loud English—his arms stay wide as they move to the side and come together when he points to the banquet hall closest to the entrance of the hotel—"out there," he says.

"Okay," Toño says. He grabs the first table and begins to carry it outside.

"Wait, wait, wait," says William as he shuffles forward to grab the bottom of the table. "Let's carry them together."

The table isn't too heavy for Toño to lift alone, but he gets the feeling William doesn't want to carry a table by himself.

Once the tables are brought out in twice as many trips as it should have taken and arranged in the banquet hall, William directs Toño to use a hand truck to bring out a stack of chairs. Eight chairs are then set around each table.

The whole process of setting up takes two hours. Toño stays busy during the three-hour graduation party serving food and clearing tables, and an hour after the party is over the tables and chairs have been stacked in the back room once more.

"All that's left is to clean the floors," William says. He disappears into the back hallway and comes back out pushing a mop in a bucket of steaming water and carrying a push broom. "I'll sweep and you mop behind me," he says.

William begins to sweep a straight line across the room. Toño holds the mop in one hand with his arm extended. At first, the mop doesn't move. Toño wonders if it's because of the weight of the water. Then, in small side-to-side motions, the mop begins to clean the floor by itself. By the time William has turned around on the other side of the room, Toño is right behind him, the mop ticking like a metronome without any effort from Toño.

William stares. "How did your wrists get so strong? There's an easier way." He takes the mop from Toño and, using both hands, his torso at forty-five degrees, shows Toño the conventional way to mop.

After mimicking William, Toño doesn't see how this could be easier than letting the mop do the work on its own. Once William has his back turned, sweeping a straight line back across the room, Toño makes the mop do the work itself, guiding it with his hand. When William gets to the far side of the room, Toño places both hands back on the mop and cleans the floor the way William showed him. The entire floor is cleaned this way, with Toño letting the mop do the work except for at the edges.

An hour after the party ends, William stands with his hands on his hips to inspect the empty, clean banquet hall. "You did good today, Antonio. How would you like to work here full time?"

CHAPTER TWENTY-FOUR

Toño CALLS New York on the first day of 1982 The phone is picked up after three rings.

"Hello?"

"Jorge? It's Toño."

"Hi, Toño. How are you?"

"I'm good." Toño gets straight to the point. "Is my room still empty? I want to move back."

Isabel has made Toño's life a living hell. Her attacks began small, underhanded remarks about how long he has stayed on her couch. By December the three roommates stopped eating any meals together, and over the last month she has outright told Toño he needs to move out and twice has thrown away his food, claiming it had spoiled. Each time she leaves the room, Benito assures Toño he can stay, to ignore her, that she just needs to vent.

"It's still empty," Jorge says.

"So can I move back?"

"You should. The water and electricity haven't been paid since you left and I'm afraid they'll be turned off."

Toño can't believe what he hears, or the businesslike tone with which Jorge tells him. "Haven't been paid? Why not?"

"They are under your name! They send the bill, I think, but I don't want to open your mail. At first I assumed you were taking care of it from Maryland, but Dolores told me otherwise. You can take care of it when you come back."

"Why would I pay those bills when I haven't even lived there in months?"

"Because they are under your name." Jorge pauses. "You can't just come back and ignore your responsibilities."

"I'm not paying for things I never used. Forget I said anything and get those transferred to you or Dolores."

"She wants to talk to you," Jorge says.

"Toño?"

"Hi, Dolores."

"Paula wanted me to tell you she misses you."

"That's nice."

"Don't you miss her too?"

Toño doesn't answer his cousin's question. "Tell her to spend more time with her man."

"She's upset you just left her. She really liked you."

"Couldn't have liked me much, she wouldn't leave her husband."

"Things aren't always so simple, Toño. Not everything is black and white."

"It should be."

"She lives across the hall from me now, we got her the apartment last month." Dolores's voice lowers to a whisper. "Her wing is healed but now both are crooked and will be for the rest of her life."

Toño can't believe Dolores knows about the real reason for the hump on Paula's back. He doesn't say a word.

"How are things with you?" Dolores asks to break the silence.

Toño tells her about his life in Maryland but leaves out the attacks from Isabel. Dolores tells Toño she hopes he finds happiness before they hang up the phone.

The memory of Jorge's attitude is enough to cause Toño to forget about Paula's message. Toño convinces himself he has been spared from a disastrous decision and resolves not to let Isabel affect him. The conversations are replaying in his mind when Benito takes a seat next to him at the kitchen table.

"I'm selling my car. Three hundred dollars and it's yours. Interested?" Benito says, pulling Toño away from his thoughts.

The car is a rusted green Oldsmobile, and Isabel has pestered Benito to upgrade since Toño moved in. "It runs okay?" Toño asks.

"Runs fine. We could get five hundred for it but since you're a friend we wanted to give you a deal."

Missing the bus has been a constant source of worry since Toño has started his job, and once, when he missed the bus, he had to run the entire way just to make it to work on time. He arrived soaked in sweat and never dried off during his shift. Three hundred dollars is a small price to pay to never have to do that again. "I'll take it," he says.

"Great! Could you have the money by Saturday morning? We are going to look at new cars in the afternoon."

"I can give it to you now," Toño says. He is about to stand up when Benito places a hand on Toño's shoulder and keeps him seated.

"Wait until Saturday, I need the car until then," Benito says.

Toño and Benito take the car around the block to make sure everything is in working order on Saturday morning. It becomes clear, to Benito and to the other drivers on the road, that Toño needs to practice driving.

"Where's Esteban been? He hasn't been around," Toño says as he makes a turn, cutting off a car in the process.

Benito's white knuckles clutch the car door from the passenger seat. "We've both been busy. Please focus on the road."

"I'm fine. This is easy!" Toño says. He swerves to avoid the curb that shifts into the road.

"You don't have a license, do you?" Benito says, his voice tinged with fear.

"No, I don't. I'll just be careful. What's the worst they can do, send me back to El Salvador? My dad said I always have a home there waiting for me."

Benito sighs. "Esteban can help you get your license. He has a friend who works in Virginia."

"Virginia? Why not Maryland?" Toño says.

Benito leans over, pulls out his wallet from his back pocket, and withdraws his own license from Virginia. "In Maryland you have to have papers. It's easier for illegals to get a license in Virginia."

"How much does it cost?"

"We have to ask Esteban. Careful, Toño!"

Toño presses the brakes much harder than necessary and the car skids to a stop. Both men lurch forward before the car runs a stop sign. Toño laughs.

"Let's go back," says Benito.

Toño turns the car around and when he gets back to the apartment parks the car at a crooked angle. Benito opens the glove compartment.

"Title's in here," Benito says. He holds the title up for Toño to see before putting it back. "I'll talk to Esteban about the license. Please don't mention it to Isabel."

"Why not?"

Benito searches the bushes outside his window for the right words. "She doesn't want me doing anything illegal."

"She doesn't care where you got your license?"

"She doesn't want me to do anything illegal anymore. I already had this when I met her. Either way, just keep your mouth shut, okay?"

Toño doesn't talk to Isabel anyways. If anything, she talks at him and he listens. "Not a problem," Toño says.

As Benito gets out of the car, Toño tells him he's going out for a drive. There are plenty of close calls, and therefore plenty of reasons to laugh. Twice he almost hits the car in front of him, and he runs a red light, the fact he was supposed to stop registering halfway through the empty intersection. Toño is so happy with his new purchase that nothing can touch his mood and therefore nothing could touch his car.

The other drivers on the road that day never forget the immigrant in the green Oldsmobile they saw breaking so many traffic laws with a wide grin on his face.

CHAPTER TWENTY-FIVE

Toño calls home in the afternoon to tell his parents about his newest purchase. After describing the car to his father, he finds out his younger brother Angel wants to talk to him.

"I want to come to the States," his brother says after more than a little small talk.

"Okay. When?"

"Maybe in a few months?"

"Good idea, you won't like this cold weather." Toño describes the effects of the change in temperature, the way the cold burrows into his core when he stands outside waiting for the bus. Angel has never been outside the tropical climate of Central America, so every detail about the cold fascinates him.

"How much money do you have saved?"

"Some, but dad said he would help me."

Toño feels a flush of red creep up his neck at the mention of the use of his father's money.

"I'll see what I can do," Toño says before hanging up the phone. Liquid runs from his nose to his upper lip and when he wipes it off he finds blood on the napkin.

Toño talks to Benito about bringing Angel to the states.

Isabel is out shopping, so the two men are alone in the apartment.

"I know Isabel wants to bring her sister Camila too," Benito says.

"We need to find a pollero to bring them across. Think Esteban knows anyone?"

"I know he does, his cousin is the one who brought him across. Let me call him."

Benito talks to the bear on the phone about bringing two people across the border and about getting Toño a license on Tuesday.

"Fifteen thousand for the pollero and Tuesday works for him," Benito says after hanging up the phone.

Esteban calls on Monday night. "Are you ready to go tomorrow?" he asks Toño.

"I'm ready. What time do you want to go?"

"Pick me up at eight."

Toño opens his mouth to say, "Will do," but the line has already gone dead. He asks Benito where Esteban lives.

"You know where the 7-Eleven is on Frederick Avenue, next to the car dealership?"

"Yes," Toño lies. He has no idea where it is but imagines it can't be hard to find.

"He'll be there. Be extra careful until you get that license!"

Toño laughs. "You got it," he says.

"Seriously, they can deport you if you get caught. I saw the way you drive. Anyone can tell that you have no business being on the road!"

"I'll be fine," Toño says.

Toño is able to find the correct store after a slow drive inspecting every car dealership for a 7-Eleven in its shadow. He pulls into a parking spot at five minutes past eight. Toño wonders what Esteban's response will be to his being a few minutes late, but when the bear gets into the car and doesn't mention it Toño decides not to apologize. He gets onto the highway and after forty-five minutes of silence, Esteban directs Toño to exit the highway onto a Virginia road. He then issues directions as if he has taken this route a million times before.

"Turn here."

"Left at the light."

"Ten minutes down this road."

"Get in the right lane."

"Up there, on your right."

Toño pulls into the parking lot of the government building and parks his car with the back corner still over the line. The two men walk inside, Toño grabs a number from the ticket machine, and they sit down on a metal bench to wait. Toño tries to engage the bear in conversation but gives up after Esteban continues to respond with one-word answers. When his number is called, the two men walk to the counter.

Before the clerk who called their number, an older white woman, is able to greet them, another clerk, a young Hispanic man, materializes behind her. He leans close to her and Toño hears him say, "I started their paperwork yesterday, you can send them over to me once I'm finished with the guy at my counter."

Toño looks down the length of the counter and sees an Asian man stare at them from across the Hispanic clerk's empty chair.

"I can take care of it," the woman who called Toño's number says.

"They only speak Spanish," the male clerk says in English. The woman looks at Toño and Esteban and is careful not to linger on the bear's furry face.

"It's true," Esteban says in English.

A quizzical look passes over the woman's face before she shrugs. "All right," she says. "Tell them to take a seat again."

In Spanish, the young man tells Toño and Esteban to sit down and he will call them in a moment. The female clerk looks at her list and calls the next number in the queue to her spot on the counter.

The clerk waves up Toño and Esteban when he finishes with his customer.

"Good to see you," he says to Esteban in Spanish.

The two men talk about mutual friends and fill each other in on the women they have each slept with while the clerk begins the process of issuing a license to Toño. Their conversation is put on pause when the clerk has to obtain Toño's information. The whole process takes less than ten minutes.

"Did he tell you the cost?" the clerk says to Toño.

Toño looks at Esteban. "It's three hundred," Esteban says.

Three hundred! Toño can't believe his ears. There is nothing he can do about it now other than be thankful he brought plenty of cash, just in case. By the way Benito talks, the license is a necessity, and without papers, this is the only way to get one.

Esteban turns to the clerk. "He knows now."

"That's how much you have to give Esteban. Twenty here, for the system."

Toño pulls out his wallet and hands over the cash.

"He'll make sure the rest gets to me," the clerk says.

Toño nods his head. Getting a car has turned out to cost way more than he expected. Every cent counts now that he knows how much it will cost to get Angel across the border, even if his brother will pay him back.

The clerk hands Toño a small piece of paper. "This is your temporary license. Keep this with you and the plastic one will be mailed to you within the next two weeks."

It takes three weeks for the license to arrive. The government envelope is inside another, larger envelope sent from an address in Virginia. When Toño looks at his license he sees that the address listed matches the one on the larger envelope. He doesn't bother to ask Esteban who lives at the Virginia address.

Toño doesn't feel any different driving, but he reminds himself it's better to be safe than sorry. Now that his brother's on his way to the country there's no reason to roll the dice and get deported for something as inconsequential as a traffic stop.

CHAPTER TWENTY-SIX

Toño takes off work on the last Saturday in April 1982. He drives down to the airport in D.C. with Benito and Isabel to pick up his brother Angel and Isabel's sister Camila. They have flown in from San Diego after crossing the border two days ago.

On his approach to the airport he continues to travel the same speed even though, unknown to him, the speed limit has decreased. He races past three cars before he realizes he is the only one weaving in and out of traffic. By then it is too late. Flashing blue-and-red lights show up in his rearview mirror.

"Do you know why I pulled you over?" the officer asks Toño from outside the driver's side window. He has Toño's license and registration in hand.

"I was going too fast," Toño admits. "I didn't see the speed limit change."

"That's right. You coming from Virginia?"

"Maryland," Benito says from the passenger seat in an effort to be helpful.

The officer raises an eyebrow.

"He's coming from Maryland, I'm coming from Virginia," Toño says.

The officer leans over and takes a long look at Benito before he looks into the back seat and inspects Isabel. He clears his throat. "What brings you to the airport today?"

"My brother's coming to visit and I'm picking him up. I haven't seen him for a long time." Toño hopes his English is clear enough for the officer to understand.

The officer studies Toño's face. His eyes fall to the license in his hand. "Bet you miss him," the officer says, his face unchanging.

"I do."

"Well, if you get in an accident then you'll never see him again." The officer hands over Toño's paperwork. "Think about that the next time you're in a rush. I'm letting you off with a warning. Slow down next time, you hear?"

"Yes, sir."

Toño pulls back into the flow of cars with a lump in his throat, careful to follow the speed of traffic until he gets to the parking lot.

"That was lucky!" Benito says when they get out of the car.

"It was," Toño says. His heartbeat returns to normal in the fresh air.

"Your license says you live in Virginia?" Isabel asks, an accusatory tone to her words.

"It's a long story," says Toño. He makes a mental note to thank Benito for insisting he get his license the next time the two men are alone.

The three of them wait outside the terminal for close to an hour before Angel walks through the gate. The two brothers recognize each other instantly; both faces break into a broad smile after years apart. A lot has changed, but anybody who saw the two of them stand next to each other would still have no doubt they are brothers.

Angel was a scrawny teenager when Toño left. Now, a full-grown man has arrived. The stubble of a few days dots Angel's youthful skin, and he has grown to be the exact same height as Toño. He remarks on Toño's thicker mustache, saying it makes him look old.

Anyone watching Isabel would witness a reunion between two women who look nothing alike. Isabel, bony and lean, has tears running down her cheeks as she embraces her sister. Camila is a head shorter and looks to have eaten all the meals Isabel missed growing up. Her round face, common among those with native blood to spare, fights back tears, and her long black hair reaches the middle of her back. When Camila lets the tears flow it becomes obvious the two of them are related. Their faces become contorted mirror images of each other and they each emit small, high-pitched squeaks with each sob. Both women bring both hands up to their faces and bend over at the same angle as their chests rise and fall in unison.

When Isabel has composed herself, she beckons Toño to come closer. "Toño, I'd like you to meet my sister Camila."

"Pleasure to meet you," Toño says with formality.

Isabel watches their introduction with the future in her eyes.

Toño feels the pressure surround his soul and realizes Benito's wife hopes he ends up falling in love, and if fate allows, the two couples can grow old together. He decides he wouldn't mind getting to know Camila better. She's pretty, in her own way, but something is off. He can't quite place his finger on it, but there is a certain amount of distance between them, a border no pollero could cross, which he attributes to nerves.

The five Salvadorans drop off the travelers' luggage at the apartment before they go out for lunch. Benito chooses to eat at a Mexican restaurant close to their house where he and Isabel are regulars. Nobody raises an objection. Everyone enjoys their meal, but Toño can't help but notice how aloof Angel has become. His brother doesn't say a word the entire meal, and unless the years have changed his brother more than he realizes, this is wrong. Two rounds of margaritas do nothing to loosen Angel's tongue.

If Toño knew Camila better, or was better at reading women, he would have noticed the furtive glances the woman casts towards his brother. Angel is doing his best to avoid her gaze, and Isabel is too busy trying to stimulate conversation to notice the object of her sister's desire.

That night, Isabel decides where the two extra bodies will sleep. It is agreed Angel will sleep on the floor, next to Toño's couch, and Camila will sleep on the floor at the foot of her bed. She doesn't have to say it, but the expectation is that Toño will move out with Angel, and Camila can take over sleeping on the couch.

Toño leaves for work the next day with enough time to stop by the McDonald's closest to the hotel before his shift begins. He asks the man at the register if they are hiring, and after he says "yes," he requests an application. The cashier retrieves his manager from the back. The manager, a middle-aged black woman, comes to the front and hands Toño a piece of paper.

"Fill this out and bring it back. We aren't hiring here, but there's a new store in Derwood that needs people," she says.

"Derwood? Where's that?" Toño asks as he folds the application twice and puts it in his pocket.

"Not far, maybe ten minutes if you have a car."

Toño pretends not to notice the woman's condescending look. "I have a car," he says with pride.

"Good for you. Like I said, ten minutes."

Toño has Angel fill out the application. They go to Derwood early on Friday to drop off the form.

"Shouldn't we find somewhere to live first?" Angel says on the drive. "Isabel doesn't like us there."

"Finding a place to live is easy, I don't want to worry about how we'll pay rent. She's always sour, that's why her cheeks are always squeezed together so tight."

Angel laughs. "I have money saved."

"Saved. No reason to dip into that if you don't have to."

Angel nods at his older brother's advice.

They walk into the Derwood McDonald's and ask the cashier to speak to a manager. A round man with a white button-down shirt emerges from the back. A ring of brown hair surrounds a shiny bald head and matches the mustache on his pink face. The cashier directs the bald man to the two brothers waiting off to the side.

"Morning, gentlemen! What can I do for you?" the manager booms.

Toño opens his mouth to speak, but Angel beats him to the first word. "I'm looking for a job."

Toño stares at his brother, surprised at how well he speaks English.

"Are you now? What's your name, son?"

"Angel."

"Rob," the manager says. The two men shake hands.

"And you? Are you looking for a job as well?" Rob says to Toño. He extends his hand. "Rob."

"Toño. And no, not me. Just him."

"Just along for the ride, eh?"

Angel hands his completed application to the manager.

"Okay, let's see what we got here," Rob says. He nods as he reviews the answers. "You can work whenever?"

"Just tell me when and I'll be here," says Angel.

"Perfect!" Rob looks Angel in the eye. "Do you have fifteen minutes to knock out a quick interview?"

Angel looks at Toño. Toño glances down at his watch and nods.

Rob provides both brothers with a complimentary drink and tells Toño to take a seat in the lobby while he and Angel sit in a booth at the back of the restaurant. The interview lasts seventeen minutes. Angel gets up from the booth and walks over to Toño, beckoning with his head for the two of them to leave. They walk in silence until Toño's curiosity gets the best of him.

"Well . . ." Toño says.

"I got the job," Angel says. He smiles without taking his eyes off the car ahead of him.

"You got the job! That's great!" Toño says.

"I guess."

"You're not happy?"

"He wants me to work all the time! It's going to be a lot of hours."

"Once you get settled into a routine it won't be so bad. Did he say when you would start?"

"Next week. On Monday."

Angel comes home from his first day of work in a terrible mood. He throws his hat on the counter and talks while Toño watches the news.

"I can't stand my boss!" Angel says.

Toño turns away from the TV. "What's wrong with him? Lazy?"

"Not Rob, this is another one. A woman. She's obsessed with work, but she has a way of getting under my skin. She makes me do things I don't want to do on purpose!"

"Like what?" Toño asks.

"Like clean the bathrooms."

"You do realize it's her job to tell you what to do, right?" Toño says.

"I can't describe it. I'm telling you, she's too much."

"She can't be that bad. What's her name?"

"Lori."

"American?"

"Of course."

"What's she look like?"

"Like a white lady? It's strange though, her skin is green."

"Like a plant?"

"Lighter than that, maybe like a plant that's never seen the sun."

Angel opens the refrigerator and emerges with a plate of leftover steak in hand. He pulls a knife and fork from the drawer and begins to eat the meat cold.

"Now that you have a job we have to start looking for somewhere else to live," Toño says after turning off the TV. "Isabel's not going to put up with us living here much longer."

CHAPTER TWENTY-SEVEN

"She's kicking me out!" Angel says over the phone. He's frantic with worry.

"What do you mean?" Toño says. It's Thursday night at the hotel and he was pulled away from his work by William.

"Isabel! She's kicking me out of the house. She found out I slept with Camila in California!" Angel then dives into an incoherent account of a night the two immigrants shared together in the hotel after they crossed the border. Toño understands the gist of the story: they are alone in a strange land and found comfort in each other's arms.

"When did she say you have to leave by?" Toño says. He feels like this is the sort of decision he should have been made a part of.

"Now! She said I have to leave now," Angel says. He chokes on his words. "Where am I supposed to go?"

"We'll figure something out. Wait for me to get back and we can figure this out."

Toño is lost in his work for the rest of his shift and doesn't reflect on the situation until the drive back home. Their rent has been paid for the month; why is she kicking his brother out for something so trivial?

Toño has to use his shoulder to open the front door against a rush of wind trying to escape. He walks through the gale and into the kitchen. Pots and pans have been flung everywhere and the flowers in the vase, fresh a week ago, lay dead and scattered on the floor. Benito sits at the kitchen table, a defeated man, while Isabel paces in front of the sink. Wind swirls around her.

"What's going on?" Toño asks.

"Your brother slept with my sister!" Isabel cries out.

"Where are they?" Toño asks Benito.

"Camila's in our room, Angel's locked himself in the bathroom," Benito says.

"Is that it?" Toño asks Isabel.

"Is that it . . . is that it! Yes, that's it! She had never been with a man before that serpent came and seduced her! I had my doubts about them coming across the border together and turns out I was right!"

Camila speaks up from the doorway and all three turn to look at her. "Calm down, Isabel," she says. "I'm not upset and you shouldn't be either. It was my choice as much as his."

"Don't tell me to calm down!" Isabel screams. Camila falls silent and stares at the floor. Toño looks at Benito: the husband must have found something more interesting at his feet because his eyes are also drawn down. They have both left Toño alone to stand up to the force of Isabel.

"Angel said you kicked him out?" Toño says. He does his best to adopt a conversational tone.

"I did! Right before he locked himself in the bathroom."

"How can you do that? I pay rent here."

"I won't have that man under my roof, sneaking around, seducing my younger sister. She came here for a better life, not to sleep with some immigrant Salvadoran!"

Toño's blood boils, but he forces himself to stay patient. "You do know we are all immigrant Salvadorans, right? Is my brother not good enough for your sister?"

"He doesn't want anything to do with her!"

"He said that?"

"In not so many words."

"They are both adults."

"I don't care!" Isabel bellows. Losing steam, she leans against the counter and crosses her arms. "He needs to be gone by this weekend."

"If he leaves, I leave."

Toño and Isabel lock eyes, each daring the other to blink.

Benito finds his voice. "Don't be like that. We can find somewhere for him to stay."

"Don't be like what?" Toño demands, losing his composure. "This is my brother. My family. You think I would let him move out without me?"

"Good, you can go too," says Isabel.

Toño stares at the enraged woman. He considers telling Benito to calm her down before he decides against it. He walks past Camila on his way to the bathroom.

Angel lets Toño in after three knocks and Toño closes the door behind him.

"Why did you do that?" he asks his brother.

"It just happened."

"Well now we have to find somewhere else to live."

"We? No! You stay here. I'll find somewhere else." Angel looks at himself in the mirror. "Maybe it was a mistake to come here."

"Don't be ridiculous. It's easy to find somewhere to live. Rooms in America are like fruit, ready to be picked whenever hunger strikes. Watch, we'll find something. Mark my words."

The next day, Toño describes the predicament to a server

named Manuel during their meal break. Manuel, the same age as Angel, is from Guatemala and has been working at the hotel for the last month. He keeps his hair buzzed, and the right arm of his glasses is kept in place with tape. "Do you have any idea where you will move to?" he asks.

"Not yet. If we need to I can get a room here until we find a place."

"So you and your brother need somewhere to stay . . ." Manuel says. He explains how there is an old man who runs a restaurant in a town up north called Braddock Heights. Attached to the restaurant are a few two-bedroom apartments, also owned by the old man, one of which is empty. The town is forty minutes away, but since Toño has a car it shouldn't be a problem to get to the hotel each day.

"I'll have to drive Angel to work each day," Toño thinks out loud.

"He could always work for him. Arminda already does," Manuel says. Manuel explains that, as part of the original arrangement with the old man, his wife, Arminda, is allowed to sleep in the unoccupied apartment because the couple only has one car and it would be hard for her to get from where they live in Gaithersburg to the restaurant each day. He takes a bite of his dinner roll and swallows before he continues. "I never wanted to move there myself because I didn't want to pay for two bedrooms, but if the two of you take one room we can take the other!"

Toño doesn't take more than a second to make his decision. "I'm in. I'll tell Angel. Think we could move in this weekend?"

"I'll tell Arminda to talk to the old man."

Manuel has an extra spring in his step for the rest of the night, and Toño is surrounded by a sense of relief. When their work is done and William has wished them a good night, they part ways and agree to discuss again at work the next day.

Isabel has locked herself in her room with Camila when Toño gets home.

"You're really moving out then?" Benito says.

"Isabel made it clear we aren't welcome."

"Only Angel has to go! I'm sure, given time, she will calm down and realize how having you pay to sleep on the couch helps us out."

"How long will that take? Weeks? Months?"

Benito doesn't say a word.

"Would you leave your brother alone?" Toño asks.

"He wouldn't be alone if he found somewhere close."

"He just got here."

"We were alone when we got here too," Benito says.

"Did you forget what it was like? I'm not doing that to him. I promised him I would bring him over, and now that he's here, he's my responsibility. If you can't understand this then we have nothing left to talk about."

At work on Saturday, Manuel tells Toño the two brothers can move in whenever they are ready, and Sunday afternoon, after work, Toño drives his big green Oldsmobile north to Braddock Heights for the first time, with Angel in the passenger seat and their belongings in the trunk. The trip takes just over forty minutes. The restaurant is just off the highway that runs north to south. The old man is at work in the restaurant, and after Toño walks inside and introduces himself, surrounded by ancient hardwood floors and walls covered with sports memorabilia, he walks back out with the key to the apartment.

The brothers choose which room they want, and since the space is unfurnished, they lay blankets down on the floor to use as beds.

Toño leaves Braddock Heights early enough on Monday morning to stop by some trash receptacles near apartment complexes in Gaithersburg. He is able to find a nightstand and a lamp, which turns out to be broken. At work he asks the servers for leads on two mattresses, and they promise to keep their eyes open.

After a late night at the hotel, Toño's heavy eyelids try their hardest to meet each other on the drive home, and he tells them to get used to it, that today wasn't so bad, because on days Angel has to work as well their day will be much longer.

CHAPTER TWENTY-EIGHT

Toño and Angel's room is furnished with dumpster finds by the time the leaves change. Toño's schedule is such that Angel will never have to work on days Toño has to arrive at the hotel early, since his brother would have no way to get from Braddock Heights to Gaithersburg. Two nights of the week Angel has to stay at McDonald's late, much later than Toño gets off work at the hotel. The day after one of these nights, Toño has off work so he is able to sleep in. The other day, Sunday, Toño has to be at the hotel early in the morning to get set up for weekend brunch. On these nights Toño is unable to get more than four hours of sleep. Toño acts like the lack of sleep doesn't affect him, but the rings around his eyes tell a different story.

One day, a Sunday late in November, Toño's car won't start. The car has gas—he never lets it get below a quarter tank—and the battery seems to work because the lights are no dimmer than usual. The engine just won't turn over.

"How about a car wash?" Toño says, thinking the vehicle might be upset about its neglected exterior. "Would you like that?" He turns the key again with no luck.

He tries to pump the gas while turning the key. Nothing.

He tries to push the brake while turning the key. Nothing. The dust on the dashboard catches his eye, so he leans forward to blow it away before turning the key again. This time, the car seems to almost start before it changes its mind.

By now Toño is worried he will be late for work. He rushes inside and grabs a paper towel, wets it with cleaning solution, and comes back outside to wipe the dashboard. He throws away the pile of trash in the cupholder. On a whim, he shakes out the driver's side mat before he gets back inside and turns the key again. After a few tense moments the engine roars to life. Toño places his forehead on the steering wheel and promises to keep the car clean in the future.

When he gets to work he finds out the person in charge of the banquet hall that night has called out sick. William should be the one to cover the shift, but Toño knows his manager spends Sunday evenings with his daughter, so he offers to stay the full day, even though he only got a few hours of sleep the night before.

Toño's dead on his feet the entire day. Two of his employees notice and offer to stay late to clean up, so after Toño makes sure the evening's event goes by without a hitch, he leaves at the conclusion of the party.

A wave of exhaustion hits Toño the second he sits down in his car. He fishes his keys from his pocket and finds the car won't start. Again. He leans back, his eyes closed and head on the headrest, and takes a second for himself.

"Just get me home," he pleads.

He turns the keys again and the car starts. Both hands rest on the steering wheel, and he widens his eyes in order to gather himself for the drive home. He backs out, leaves the hotel parking lot, and gets onto the highway. He can feel himself become hypnotized by the rear lights ahead of him and shakes his head in order to break their spell. It takes all of his strength to keep his eyelids apart. He rolls down the window, hoping the fresh air will help keep him awake. Twice he drifts into lanes on either side of him, and each time he returns to the proper lane he crosses himself, thanking God the streets are empty at this time of night.

He gets off the highway at his exit. The traffic light to get onto the road home is red, and sleep visits him as he waits. A honk behind Toño wakes him up and he sticks his hand up between the two front seats, hopeful the driver behind him can see the gesture through his rear window.

"Only a few more minutes," he says to himself. He begins to count the seconds as they pass and turns on the interior light to keep an eye on the time, switching his focus between the road ahead of him and the clock as he gets closer to home. The length of time a minute takes keeps changing on him, some fast and some slow. Sometimes he is into the seventies before the clock displays a new minute, and three times in a row his count is still in the forties.

"This isn't good," he says. Either his counting has slowed down or he is losing time as his blinks get longer and longer. He redoubles his focus. "Not much longer now."

"One, two, three . . ." Toño says to the air around him. The next thing he knows, his eyes open and he sees two headlights in front of him. The van ahead is two car lengths away, the distance between them closing fast as both vehicles race forward. Toño is frozen, wondering if this is what it feels like to be in a dream. The car takes control and swerves; the rush of wind through the window ruffles Toño's hair as the van passes. He braces himself in case the van hits the tail end of his big Oldsmobile. The car rattles from how closely the two vehicles pass each other.

Toño looks at the clock and watches a new minute begin. "Four," he says. Realizing how much time he lost, he slaps himself in the face. The rest of the drive back home is spent wide awake with adrenaline, cursing the driver of the van for not honking his horn and alerting him that he had been driving on the wrong side of the road. He gets home and parks the car, grateful to still be alive. He collapses into bed and falls asleep without even bothering to take off his clothes.

The sound of clanging dishes wakes Toño up the next morning. Toño pries himself from bed and walks into the kitchen, leaving an imprint of sweat where his body had been.

"Morning!" Angel says. He already has his work uniform on, black pants and a short-sleeved white button-down, and is eating a bowl of cereal.

"Good morning," Toño mutters. He searches the kitchen, wondering why his brother made so much noise. It turns out most of their dishes—three bowls and four plates—are dirty in the sink. His brother must have had to clean one of the bowls and in the process woken Toño up. Good thing too, they have to leave soon, and as it is, Toño will have to rush to get ready on time.

From inside a fortress of empty Coke cans and beer bottles, Toño grabs an overripe banana for breakfast. He rearranges Styrofoam takeout containers from the previous week to make room for himself and leans on the counter.

"Tired?" Angel asks.

Toño nods. "I'm starting to lose track of time," he says.

CHAPTER TWENTY-NINE

When the old man informs Arminda she won't have as many hours at the restaurant in the spring. she asks Angel to get her a job at McDonald's. At first Toño feels like he will be taken advantage of, that he will have to make the drive to Gaithersburg more often, but Arminda and Manuel assure him this isn't the case.

"If anything, it will make your life easier!" Arminda says. "Manuel and I have a car too, we can help make sure Angel gets to and from work. You need to sleep more, the circles around your eyes make you look like a raccoon."

Summer rolls around and finds all four members of the apartment in Braddock Heights focused on their work. Manuel works as a landscaper during the week and is still working at the hotel with Toño on Friday nights and Sunday mornings. Angel and Arminda have set schedules, so their trips can be arranged ahead of time with the two cars available.

Angel comes home in a terrible mood one night at the end of July. He and Arminda have just closed the store together, and she follows him through the front door. He throws his hat on the couch while his brother watches the news.

"You closed with her again, didn't you?" Toño says. Angel comes home in a bad mood whenever he works with Lori.

"She's not so bad, you just have to do what she says. You'd like her," Arminda says to Toño.

Toño laughs. "I want to see her."

"You're not missing much," Angel says.

"Well I've never seen a woman with green skin!"

"I'm working with her tomorrow night, come visit then," says Arminda.

"Will you be there?" Toño asks Angel.

"No, I have off tomorrow. Thank God."

Toño thinks about his own schedule. Tomorrow is Tuesday, his day off, and all he has to do is laundry. "I could take you to work," he says.

"I start work at two. Come in, grab lunch, and I'll point her out to you," says Arminda.

Toño spends the rest of the night with Arminda's words ringing in his head: "You'd like her." If she is American she could help him get his citizenship instead of him going through the tedious process of getting his green card on his own.

If they were to get married, if he ever wanted to stay.

The Derwood McDonald's has a short line in front of the register when he drops off Arminda. He surveys the menu even though he orders the same thing every time: a Big Mac, fries, and a Coke. Arminda comes back out from the kitchen with a rag in hand and walks into the lobby from behind the counter.

"Come with me," she says.

Toño follows his friend as she wipes down all the tables and cleans up ketchup from the condiment station. "She's in the back counting money right now. She'll come out front when she's done."

Arminda finishes cleaning and goes behind the counter. Toño stands in the back of the line, the fifth person back.

Arminda and the other cashier go to work clearing the line. An American woman, midtwenties, comes from the kitchen when Toño is the next in line to place his order. She has on a white button-down shirt and the serious face all managers wear when there is work to be done. Her skin is pale green.

Arminda motions with her eyes to Toño that this is the woman he has come to see. Toño thinks she is pretty in an American sort of way. Her movements reveal the strength of her body, and her brown eyes search the room to make sure everything about her domain aligns with her expectations.

The other cashier finishes with his customer before Arminda finishes with hers and calls Toño to the front. Arminda tells the other cashier to let her take this one because he is her friend. Lori's ears perk up at this news. She approaches Arminda at the register and tells her to make sure this "friend" is being charged for everything he orders.

Arminda smiles and nods.

Toño walks forward when Arminda finishes with her customer. Lori pretends to be stocking straws in the area. Before Toño can order any food Arminda says, "Lori, I'd like you to meet Angel's brother Toño."

A look of disgust flashes across Lori's face before it's replaced by a smile that extends from the corners of her lips to the corners of her eyes. "It's nice to meet you," she says.

"Same," Toño says. Lori stares at him, waiting for him to say something, anything, but no more words come from his lips.

"What do you want for lunch, Toño?" Arminda asks.

Toño orders his usual. Lori makes sure to mention to Arminda that since Angel isn't here Toño isn't eligible to receive the family discount.

"You don't mind, do you, Toño?" Arminda says.

"Not at all." He hands over exact change then steps to the side. Thoughts of his hunger get buried beneath questions about why this American woman cares so much about a few cents. He has no problem paying, but Lori has made such a big deal about the discount that Toño begins to think she might not like Hispanic people.

When a destitute-looking white family ordering food from the other cashier tries to use an expired coupon and Lori tells them the coupon can't be accepted, Toño realizes she acts like this to all customers, regardless of race.

Arminda brings Toño's tray of food over herself. "I told Lori you want her number," she says with a mischievous grin.

Toño laughs to hide his embarrassment. "What did you do that for?"

"Why not? She's single. You can take her out, show her a good time."

Toño knows Angel wouldn't like it if he were to take her out, but he wonders if maybe she acts so sour because she's so alone.

"What did she say?"

"She said, 'If he wants it tell him to come get it himself!' That woman makes me laugh," Arminda says, shaking her head with a laugh.

"You think I should?"

"Why not? A nice American woman could be good for you!"

"I'll think about it," Toño says. He takes his tray and sits down next to a back window. He watches Lori while he eats, unsure of whether or not he should pursue. He enjoys witnessing the command she radiates over her employees. It isn't mean, just ruthless. Not overbearing, but thorough.

"She didn't say no," he says to himself as he chews his burger. "But Angel can't stand her!" He shovels a handful of fries into his mouth.

Lori walks into the lobby with a rag in her hand. She wipes the tables around Toño and takes a long time at the condiment bar, well within talking distance of where Toño is seated.

Toño stops eating and watches Lori clean. Her full figure moves in unison as she cleans the counter, and he imagines himself behind her in the middle of the night. In this moment the decision is made to get her number, but the message isn't relayed to his mouth in time. She walks away without him having uttered a word.

The line is much shorter on Toño's way out. He stands near the counter to wait for his chance.

Lori notices Toño standing alone and makes sure her work takes her near him. She busies herself rearranging cups right in front of where he stands.

"Lori, right?" Toño says.

"That's me," she says with a smile.

"I'm Angel's older brother."

"I know."

A moment of silence passes between the two of them. "Would you give me your number? I'd like to take you out sometime."

"Sometime when?"

"Sometime next week."

"When next week?"

"Tuesday night?"

"I work Tuesday night."

Toño thinks. "How about Wednesday?"

"You don't like the weekends?"

"I work on the weekends."

Lori rips off a piece of receipt paper. "Wednesday night works for me. Here's my number, give me a call to let me know about the details." She rushes off to take care of some task in the kitchen only she knows about.

Toño takes the paper, exhausted from the rapid barrage of

questions. He folds the paper twice and places it next to the cash in his wallet. "This woman doesn't play around!" he says to himself in the car on the way back to Braddock Heights.

When Arminda gets home, she tells Toño she's overjoyed at the news. Manuel smiles as if he knew all along, and Angel, to his credit, pretends to be happy. "Maybe a night with you will calm her down," the brother says.

CHAPTER THIRTY

Toño CALLS Lori on Sunday night. She answers on the third ring.

"Hello?"

"It's me, Toño."

"Hi, Toño. Did you decide where we are going?" Lori says. She doesn't waste any time, and Toño feels lucky he has gotten her to slow down long enough to talk to him.

"Do you know Chi-Chi's? It's a restaurant in the mall."

"I know the place. Mexican food. Is that where you want to take me?"

"Yes, it is."

"Great! What time should I be there?"

Toño tells her he can pick her up at seven.

"No thanks, I'll drive myself," she says. "What time do you want me to meet you? Seven?"

Toño nods, hears silence, then says, "Yes."

"I'll see you at seven," she says.

Toño shows up at Chi-Chi's half an hour early. He tries to put his name in, telling the hostess his date will be there soon, but he is told there is nothing they can do without the other member of his party. Toño asks to use the restroom and is directed to the back. On his way out, he notices how many empty tables there are. The wait shouldn't be long.

Lori shows up right at seven, as if she waited in her car until the exact moment she had to come inside, at which point she did. She has on a loose-fitting summer dress and white sandals. A flush of red creeps up her neck when she sees Toño wearing a pair of worn-out jeans and a faded yellow T-shirt.

They hug and Toño walks up to the hostess, proud to tell her his date has arrived.

The hostess sings a different tune once she sees Toño's date is a white woman, her smile no longer forced, eager to help. She takes them to a table near the bar.

"Do you mind if we sit in a booth?" Lori asks Toño.

Toño shrugs and shakes his head.

"Can we have a booth?" Lori asks the hostess.

"Of course. Right this way."

The booth they are taken to is near the restrooms. "Sorry to be such a bother, but could we have one of those other empty booths, not near the bathrooms?"

"Sure, why don't you pick the one you want," the hostess says, flashing her teeth.

Lori leads them to a booth near the front of the restaurant. The other diners stare at the three of them in silence, and it isn't until they are seated that meals resume around the restaurant.

Toño orders a Coke and Lori orders a diet. They split two baskets of chips and salsa. When the waiter returns to take their orders, Toño gets carne asada with rice and Lori gets a salad with chicken.

Toño has trouble keeping up with the speed of Lori's English and defaults to one-word responses with a heavy Spanish accent whenever she asks him a question. Lori loves to talk about herself, and it doesn't take Toño long to learn to ask questions in order to keep the conversation alive. Not talking about himself doesn't bother Toño in the slightest. Truth be told, he is happy just to be seen on a date with a white woman. Here he is, the immigrant from El Salvador, with a strong American woman. Just the two of them. As she talks and talks about her childhood, and then her career, he envisions what a future with her would look like. His son would grow up as an American, a real American, not a Hispanic born on American soil. If he decides to stay.

Toño finds out Lori lives with her mother in Damascus, her commute to the Derwood McDonald's takes half an hour, and that she just bought an apartment in Germantown in order to be closer to work but hasn't gotten a bed yet. He decides to make more money and get a place of his own in order to win this woman over.

Lori offers slight resistance when Toño informs her he will take care of the bill. After he insists, she gives in without another word. The two of them leave the restaurant, and Toño floats inches above the ground on miniature clouds, lost in thoughts of the future and torn between whether or not she would go back to El Salvador with him. His new height gives him the confidence to stand outside Lori's car and ask her if she would invite him over to her place.

"On the first date? No way, Jose."

Toño feels a flash of jealousy. Why would this woman agree to a date with him if she has another man? "Jose? Who's Jose?"

"Nobody, it's a figure of speech."

"So you don't know Jose," Toño says, trying to wrap his mind around the concept.

"No, I've never met Jose!" Lori laughs and places a hand on Toño's shoulder.

Toño jerks away. "Then why would you say his name?" he accuses.

"I said it because it rhymes! Way, Jose . . . see how they sound the same?"

"I don't get it," Toño says.

Lori spends the next ten minutes trying to get her date to understand, and Toño realizes the night is over after he comes to a tentative understanding about the nature of Lori's relationship with the mysterious Jose. "Maybe you can invite me over to your place next time?"

Lori feels the thrill that comes from being desired deep within her chest. "Next time? Do you have an idea when you want the next time to be?"

Toño smells blood. "Tomorrow night I get off work at nine, is that too late?"

"Too late? Try too soon! Two days in a row, that's a lot. What makes you think I had a good enough time for that?"

The pained look on Toño's face gives his hurt away. "You didn't enjoy yourself?"

"No, I did! I was being sarcastic. I'd love to do tomorrow but I work."

Toño doesn't say a word and looks at the ground. Lori uses a finger to lift his face, looking for a sign.

"Your eyes get so blue," she says.

"They're not blue, they're brown."

"Blue like sad. Reminds me of a puppy." They stare into each other's eyes for another moment before Lori snaps the two of them from their reverie.

"We're going to have to figure out this language barrier thing!" Lori says with a smile, rubbing his shoulder. "I'm not used to being careful with my words."

Toño laughs and tells Lori the next time he can take her out is Sunday.

"Sunday it is," Lori says.

The two of them hug goodbye and Lori gets into her car. Toño watches her drive away, wishing he was going with her.

CHAPTER THIRTY-ONE

IT TAKES Toño ten minutes to get to her neighborhood from the hotel and another five to find the correct unit after work on Sunday night. The numbers of the buildings aren't displayed in plain view, and he finds her place when he recognizes her car out front.

Toño honks and Lori comes down.

"You could have come up and knocked on my door. That's what any normal person would do!" Lori says, annoyed but playful.

Toño can't tell if she is upset or not. "Sorry," he says.

"It's fine. Listen, I had an idea. What if we run to the grocery store and I make us dinner tonight?"

"I thought we could go to Chi-Chi's again. I liked it last time."

"I don't want Mexican again. Let's go to the grocery store, I'll tell you where to go."

Toño drives his big green Oldsmobile while Lori navigates. She tells him which lane to drive in, when to speed up, when to slow down, and when to stop. At red lights the car rumbles as if it will stall, but as soon as the light turns green the car runs as if there are no problems at all.

Lori doesn't believe Toño when he says he has never been in an accident. "Not even a fender bender?" she says as they pull into the parking lot.

"A what?" Toño says.

"A fender bender. A small accident."

"Why don't you just call it a small accident?" Toño says with a laugh. "And no, not even one of those." He turns into the parking space, puts the car in park, and kills the engine.

"You're going to leave the car like this?" Lori asks. She opens the door and looks at the painted line. "You aren't straight at all!"

"Oh well," Toño says. He opens his door and begins to get out of the car.

Lori leans over the center console and looks up at Toño. "You don't want to straighten it?"

"You think I should?"

"Yes."

"All right, hold on." He gets back into the car, Lori shuts her door, and after the car is convinced to start he straightens it in the parking spot. "Good?" Toño says when the job is done.

"Perfect," Lori says. She reaches over and puts her hand behind Toño's head, her fingers surrounding his neck.

It hasn't taken long for Toño to learn the best way to get into Lori's good graces is to do what she suggests.

"What should we get?" Lori asks while they walk through the butcher section of the grocery store.

"Wings," Toño says.

"Wings? That's random. I can do wings though."

In addition to wings, Lori grabs fries, celery, and barbecue sauce. "I don't like spicy foods," she says.

Lori talks about work on the ride back to her apartment, never once asking Toño about himself. Toño is happy to listen to her talk, since his limited English doesn't lend itself to stories about the hotel.

"How do you like working with Angel?" Toño asks while they unpack the groceries in her kitchen. Her living room is empty, but the corner of a made bed can be seen through the bedroom door.

Lori preheats the oven. "He's not the best, but at least he shows up on time and never misses a shift!"

"Not the best?"

"It's hard to get him to do things he doesn't want to do."

"Sounds like Angel. In El Salvador he would only do the chores he wanted."

"That doesn't surprise me one bit," Lori says while placing the wings on a baking tray. She pulls out a cutting board and chops the celery, by hand, and Toño wonders why she doesn't tell the knife to do the work without her.

Toño tells Lori about his family, the farm, and his friends growing up. When he talks about the town's soccer team, the Deers, his gestures become more animated and he talks with his entire body.

Lori spreads the fries on a second baking tray and places both into the oven. "And the team still exists?" she says, crunching down on a piece of celery.

Toño grabs himself a cut stalk. "It does. Alfonso plays for them now," he says between crunchy bites.

"You should be proud of starting something that's lasted for so long!"

"It was just for fun," Toño says.

When the wings are done, Lori puts them into a pot and covers them with barbecue sauce. She stirs the wings with a wooden spoon and rushes to get the fries from the oven before they burn. Toño wonders why she doesn't have the spoon toss the wings by itself and realizes she hasn't trained any of her utensils. He admires how hard she has to work to cook their meal.

They eat at the counter, standing up. "How long has it been since you've been in a relationship?" Lori asks while they eat.

Toño doesn't know if what he had with Paula counts as a relationship, but since she was his last woman he tells Lori his last was in New York, almost a year ago.

"My last one ended two months ago," she says.

The knot in Toño's stomach makes it hard for him to swallow the three fries he stuffed into his mouth a moment earlier.

"He wanted me to go to college and get a degree," Lori continues. She takes a bite of a drumette and stares through her rear window, off into the night. "When I told him I didn't want to, he decided I wasn't worth his time."

Toño nods, still struggling to swallow.

"He tries to call every so often but I refuse to see him. I don't want to be with someone who cares so much about a stupid piece of paper."

"The one in New York was obsessed with a green card," Toño says when he manages to swallow. He isn't used to sharing details about Paula with anyone, let alone with the woman he pursues. "That's why we stopped."

"All she cared about is a stupid piece of paper too!"

The knot in Toño's stomach slips away but the feeling doesn't register. All he can think about is how well he aligns with the woman in front of him.

After their meal, Lori puts all the dishes into the sink to soak, the sponge lifeless behind the faucet, and apologizes for not having anywhere to sit.

"You got a bed before you got a table and chairs," Toño says with a laugh.

"I knew I wanted you to come over," she says.

Toño looks at her and smiles, glad they are on the same page.

CHAPTER THIRTY-TWO

LORI RECEIVES an assignment to help open a new McDonald's in Myersville, a town close to where Toño lives in Braddock Heights, at the end of October. She has to wake up an hour and a half earlier than normal in order to give herself enough time to get to the store, a full hour north from her apartment in Germantown. Toño offers to let her sleep at his place, but since he shares a room with his brother, she doesn't want to impose.

Toño visits the new McDonald's on one of his off days a few weeks after the store opens. He finds an exhausted Lori hunched over a broken cash register. The lunch rush has ended, but there are still a few people in line.

"I called the crew to come fix it this morning and they still aren't here!" Lori says, exasperated.

"Hello to you too," Toño says.

"Sorry, hi." She leans over the counter and gives Toño a kiss then scratches her upper lip where Toño's mustache has brushed against it. "It's been one hell of a day. How's yours been?"

"Been good. I wanted a Big Mac for lunch so I figured I'd come get one," Toño says.

"A Big Mac again? You must really like that sandwich!" Lori walks to a functional register and rings up his order, no discounts applied.

"Oh, I love it! I want to spend the rest of my life with it," Toño says. He pulls out his wallet and counts the necessary cash. He looks up to hand over his bills and finds Lori staring at him.

"The rest of your life?"

"Yes," Toño says with a laugh.

"With a sandwich?"

"With you."

Lori's knees buckle, and she uses the counter to keep herself upright. She smiles and takes Toño's cash from him. The smile stays in place as she counts his change and hands it to him.

"How do you know the sandwich wants to see you every day for the rest of their lives?"

"I don't," Toño says, pocketing his change. "But I can hope!"

Toño sits down to eat at a booth with a view of the front counter. He locks eyes with Lori and smirks between bites of his sandwich. Lori looks away with flushed cheeks every time. He wonders how a Big Mac would taste every day for the rest of his life and can't envision a future where he would ever get tired of the sandwich, even thirty-plus years in the future.

Lori's smile lasts well after Toño leaves. It lasts through the workers arriving to fix the register as she is about to get off, through her coworker telling her to "not bring her foreigner over here anymore," and through her drive home while she sits in traffic. On the phone later that night she tells Toño, "You know, I don't think I would mind a Big Mac for the rest of my life either." She refers to Toño as her fiancé from that day on.

The new designation doesn't register with Toño; he has never heard the term before. But when he overhears Lori invite her mother to dinner with her and her new fiancé, he asks what the word means after she hangs up the phone.

"It means we are engaged to be married!" Lori says.

Toño is ecstatic to hear she has agreed. He can't wait to begin his life with her and imagines what life might be like with her on a farm in El Salvador.

They show up at Betty's house in Damascus, a town twenty minutes north of Lori's apartment, at five on Sunday night. Lori has a key and lets herself in; Toño follows behind. "Mom, we're here!" she yells when they walk inside.

"I'll be right down!"

Lori and Toño sit down on the couch in the living room.

Betty walks down the stairs a few minutes later, her hair curled and wearing a floral dress. Her white necklace matches her white earrings, and Toño notices her left ring finger is bare. Toño stands up from the couch.

"Mom, this is Antonio. Antonio, I'd like you to meet my mom, Betty."

Toño extends his hand and Betty goes in for the hug. "It's so nice to meet you!" Betty says.

Toño can tell she means it.

Betty holds her future son-in-law at arm's length to inspect him. "You did good for yourself!" she says to her daughter.

"Stop it, Mom!" Lori says, embarrassed.

Toño laughs.

"Where are we going for dinner?" Betty asks.

"McDonald's?" Toño jokes.

Mother and daughter both laugh.

"How about the steakhouse in Shady Grove?" Betty says.

Lori looks at Toño. "Does that work for you?"

"Let's go!" Toño says with a nod.

Betty and Lori discuss the wedding during dinner. Toño

enjoys hearing how excited his bride-to-be gets when she talks about the wedding and is content to listen to the two women.

"Have you told your father?"

"I called him yesterday."

"What did he say?"

"He was happy at first but only until he found out Toño isn't American."

Betty shakes her head.

Lori struggles with her words. "He said not to expect him to be around if I marry a nigger."

Betty looks at Toño, who chews his steak.

"He isn't even black," Betty says.

"I tried to tell him that but you know how Dad is. Everyone not white is black."

"Well screw him then! You don't need that in your life, honey."

"I know, but it still hurts." Lori slides closer to Toño on their side of the booth, but Toño is too focused on his meal to offer support.

"On a lighter note: what about kids! Have you talked about it yet?" Betty asks the couple.

"I want one son," Toño says.

"Son? Just one?" Lori says.

"I've always imagined I'd have a son," Toño replies.

"This is something we will have to talk about," says Lori with a chuckle.

Betty is overjoyed at the thought of a grandchild; whether it's one or however many her daughter has in mind doesn't matter to her. She promises to do as much as she can over the coming months to get the wedding planned and over with so Lori and Toño can begin their family.

Toño takes care of the check and the three of them drive north to drop Betty off at home.

Betty reaches forward from the back seat and squeezes Toño's shoulder. "Thank you so much for dinner, Antonio, it was lovely," she says.

"Thanks for coming," Toño says.

On the drive back to Lori's apartment to pick up Toño's big green Oldsmobile, Lori tells Toño he can spend the night if he wants, but she has to work early the next day. "Sorry if I wake you up," she says.

"Angel is sleeping at his woman's house tonight. Why don't you sleep at my place?"

Lori agrees, packs a bag, and the two of them drive forty-five minutes north to Braddock Heights.

The apartment is silent when they walk inside; Arminda and Manuel must have already gone to bed. Lori puts her bag on Toño's bed and sits down on the couch in the living room next to Toño to watch TV before they go to bed. She is in the middle of telling him about the rest of the conversation with her dad when she jumps up and shakes her arm around as if it's been burned.

"Oh my God!" she half screams, half retches. She alternates jumping on one leg and then the other as if the carpet beneath her is hot lava. "You have roaches!" she says, her voice dripping with disgust. She points to the ground. "That was on my wrist!" Lori says.

The roach is unlike any either have ever seen, its exoskeleton dark brown with golden stripes and body larger than any watch she would ever wear.

A loud crunch fills the room, and pieces of the roach squirt out from both sides of Toño's size-nine shoe. He lifts up his foot, doesn't see the flat insect on the ground, and wipes the remnants of the bug off his shoe onto the carpet next to its juices.

"That's. So. Gross!" Lori says, turning her eyes away and holding her mouth shut against the vomit trying to escape.

"It's dead now," Toño says. He sits back down.

"You're just going to leave it there?" Lori asks.

"Think I should clean it up?"

"Obviously!"

Toño grabs a napkin from the kitchen and wipes the crushed insect from the floor. After he throws the wad away, he hears Lori yell from the living room, "Make sure you wash your hands!" He smiles and shakes his head as he goes to the sink.

In bed, Lori tells Toño she will spend the night tonight, but "that's it!"

"Because of the bug?"

"Yes, because of the bug! Did you see how big that thing was?"

"It's dead now."

"I know, but where there's one there's more."

"I had no idea you were so clean," Toño says.

"Clean! This has nothing to do with me being clean. More like I'm just not disgusting."

"So I'll have to come over to your place from now on?"

"That's right."

"Shit, I might as well move in."

Lori is silent. If it wasn't dark, she would have been able to see Toño's face and tell his offhand comment wasn't serious. "You want to move in together?" she says. Her intent was for this to be a question about his desires, not a request to cohabitate, but the language barrier between them is enough to blur the difference.

The question doesn't linger for more than a second before he agrees.

CHAPTER THIRTY-THREE

ANGEL DOESN'T TAKE the news of Toño's move well. He threatens to move back to El Salvador. "You want to live with her? There's no way I can pay rent here by myself!" he says.

"We'll find you a roommate," Toño says. Years of experience with Angel have taught him to stay calm when his brother is upset.

"You act like it's so easy! We're so far away from everything. Plus, I don't want to share a room with just anyone."

"It won't be just anyone, I promise. I won't leave until we find someone you won't mind living with. How does that sound?"

Angel sits down at the edge of his bed. "Why her? You know I can't stand her. I don't know how you can!"

"I don't know what to tell you. It just works. We're going to get married."

Angel stares at Toño with his mouth wide open. "I'll never understand it," he says. He looks around the room, at the furniture that almost all belongs to Toño. Not only will he lose his brother, he will also lose a lamp, a fan, a radio, and his dresser.

Toño guesses what's on Angel's mind and stops his brother

from taking inventory before he becomes upset again. "You can keep most of the stuff, she already has everything we need. She was planning to live by herself."

In Lori's apartment that night, Toño tells Lori he will keep his half of the room in Braddock Heights in order to help his brother with rent. "Angel wasn't happy when I told him I was moving out."

"He's never happy," Lori says. She pulls a key out of her purse. "Here, I had this made for you," she says. It's the middle of November, over three months into their relationship, and Toño now has a key to Lori's apartment.

Over dinner, Lori admits she has been thinking about something Toño said at dinner with her mom. "You only want one son?"

"That's what I had in mind. One boy, with my name, who I can tell everything to. No secrets."

"What if the first one is a girl?"

"Then we'd have one daughter! Either way, I want them to know everything that happens in the family. In El Salvador there are topics children don't hear about. Things like money. I don't want it to be like that."

"It doesn't have to be, we can raise our children however we want. But there will be more than one."

Something about the way Lori says this tells Toño this isn't up for debate. "How many do you want?"

"Six."

"Six! That's way too many. There's not enough money for six." He remembers the conversation about the optimal number of children he had with Manuel in New York. "What about three?"

Lori thinks for a moment. "Three is a good number. Maybe two boys and one girl?"

"However they come out," Toño says. Deep down he'd

prefer to have all boys, but he knows the decision is up to God, not him.

"Children need love, not money. We can face each challenge as it comes."

Toño laughs. "Six is just too many. Though they would be useful on the farm."

"Who's going to a farm?"

"We are! I only came to America to make money; the plan is to go back and start a farm."

Lori stares at Toño. "You're serious?"

"Five years, that's what I told myself when I left."

"When were you planning to tell me you were leaving?"

By now both of them have set down their silverware, the conversation taking precedent over the meal.

"I thought you would come with me," Toño says, his confused eyes giving away how he feels about her reluctance.

"To that shithole country? No way." She picks up her fork and takes a bite of her mac and cheese.

"That country is my home."

"I'm not stepping foot in El Salvador. We'll get married and stay here. I'll help you get your green card."

Toño slams a fist on the table. "I don't want to get my green card! Why do people care so much about a piece of paper?"

The fire in Lori's eyes could melt ice. "Don't ever lose your temper with me. My mother put up with abusive men and I'll be damned if I do the same!"

After a few tense minutes staring at each other, the heat from their glares heating up the food on the table, Toño tells Lori he's going back to El Salvador with or without her.

"It's going to be without me," Lori says in defiance.

"Fine." Toño stands up from the table, his meal half-finished, and grabs his bag from the bedroom that went from hers to theirs and back again in the span of a day.

Lori is still seated at the table when Toño asks if her mind is made up.

"I'm never going to El Salvador," she says.

With sadness, Toño reaches into his pocket and takes out the single key that Lori had given him earlier. He tosses it onto the table. "Goodbye then," Toño says.

He walks from the room, half hoping Lori would call him back.

He walks to his car, half hoping Lori would rush out to stop him.

He climbs into his car, half hoping he would see Lori in the rearview mirror trying to continue their argument.

The big green Oldsmobile doesn't start. Toño tries to turn the key again, but the engine refuses to turn over. An hour passes with Toño in the driver's seat wondering what to do. He catches his own reflection in the rearview mirror.

"Maybe it wouldn't be so bad to stay. If she won't go back with me I could always go visit by myself," he says to himself.

Toño's about to open the door and get out, to knock on Lori's door and walk back into her life, when he tries to start the car one more time.

The engine turns over, and Toño takes it as a sign he should drive away, not realizing the car decided to start because its driver is thinking with some sense for the first time since the argument with his former fiancé began.

CHAPTER THIRTY-FOUR

"WE HEARD YOU'RE MOVING OUT," Arminda says when Toño walks through the front door after his reflective drive home. "I can hear wedding bells already!"

Toño manages a weak smile. "After I find someone to take my half of the room," he says.

"That's what Angel said. I'm happy for you, Toño," Arminda says as she gives Toño a hug.

"Congrats," Manuel says.

Toño walks with his bag into his bedroom, thankful neither of the other two roommates asked why he came home so late at night.

"I thought you were staying at her place tonight," Angel says.

"We're finished."

"What do you mean?"

"I mean we're done. Through. Over. I told her I wanted to move back to El Salvador and she said she will never go."

"Well of course she said that; she's American! I thought you changed your mind about going back, that was why you were with her."

Toño sits down on his bed and doesn't say a word.

"So you aren't moving out anymore?" Angel asks, his voice awkward in the room as if it doesn't want to take up space.

"I am."

"But you said you broke up with Lori . . ."

"I'm going back to El Salvador."

Angel pretends he doesn't care, but Toño can hear the shock in his voice. "Is your mind made up?"

"It is. This was always the plan, to work in America for a few years, save as much money as I could, then go back to start my farm and family."

"I thought the plan was to find a wife. And what about the war?"

"Once I have the farm, women will come. What can I offer them now? I don't have anything. And the war doesn't worry me, I have nothing to do with either side."

Angel nods. "Okay, Toño, sounds like you've thought this through."

"I have." Toño then asks Angel to hold on to ten thousand dollars for him. He says it's in case he wants to come back, but really he wants Angel to have easy access to enough cash to help him in any situation. "You can always send me the money later."

Angel smiles. "Of course I'll hold onto it. It'll be waiting for you when you get back."

Toño doesn't notice the phrasing of Angel's statement. He goes to bed content with his decision, his future just a plane ride away.

Toño calls his father in San Ramon on a Tuesday morning at the end of November. After their usual small talk about their lives, Toño asks the question, in the form of a statement, which has been weighing on his mind.

"I'm ready to move back home," he says.

Jose Angel pauses on the other end of the line before he

says, "Toño, things are different now. People are killed out in the open."

"I don't want anything to do with those people. That's their problem. I just want to live on the farm and start my family."

"I understand, but both the government and the guerrillas kill people for no reason. Everyone lives in fear. We have to be careful about what we say at all times, even around neighbors we have known forever."

Toño doubles over from a sudden pain in his stomach. The sensation reminds him of when he was younger and Beto had punched him in the gut, clearing all the wind from his lungs. All this time his plan has been to return to his home. The thought kept him going through years of hard work. He has sacrificed time, money, and Lori. "Are you saying I can't come home?" he croaks.

"Of course not! I just want you to know that home isn't the same as you remember."

"So you don't mind if I buy a plane ticket and move back?"

Jose Angel sighs. "No, Toño, I don't mind at all. It will be nice having you around again."

Toño sits up straight. "Good, I'll figure out when I can leave. Angel should be fine here. He has a good job, and the Salvadoran couple we live with can make sure to help him in case he gets into trouble."

Toño and his father say their goodbyes and hang up the phone.

A travel agency near the hotel helps Toño purchase a plane ticket for the first week of December. He tells the hotel he is going to take a few weeks off to visit El Salvador, knowing the whole time he doesn't intend to return. He finds someone to take his spot in the room within a week, a worker at the hotel named Napoleon who needs a place to live. Napoleon has a car, so the distance won't be a problem. Before Toño offers him the room, he invites both Napoleon and Angel out for drinks. The two of them seem to get along, and later that night, when he is alone with his brother, Toño talks to Angel about living with Napoleon.

"He seems all right," Angel says.

"So you wouldn't mind him moving in?"

"No, that's fine. I know you want to leave, I can tell how miserable you are without your woman. If it makes you feel any better, she's miserable too. Everyone can tell, even though she tries to hide it."

It does make him feel better.

Toño has two suitcases full of luggage when Angel drops him off at the airport. He has left his winter clothes for his brother to use since he will have no need for them in the tropical climate. Angel also gets the big green Oldsmobile, troubles and all.

Neither brother has many words to say during their good-bye. Angel utters the usual, "Have a good trip," and "Tell everyone I say hi," while Toño reminds his brother to put oil in the car and stay out of trouble. Toño turns to walk into the terminal, and Angel calls out one final question.

"What about the money you wanted me to hold on to for you? You never gave it to me."

"It's in an envelope in the top dresser drawer. If you need to borrow any of it just call me first, okay?"

"I'll keep a hold of it until you get back," Angel says.

In the darkness of the drawer, the dead presidents wonder on which side of the border they will see Toño again.

PART 4

HELL AND BACK

CHAPTER THIRTY-FIVE

Toño walks off the plane in San Salvador and is hit by the heat of his country on the jet bridge into the airport. The air is less humid than in D.C. But, since the heat is constant all year long, there is a smell in the air that never goes away. A sweet mixture of sweat, ripeness, and decay.

A hand grabs Toño's right shoulder as he stands next to the baggage claim waiting for his luggage to emerge from the depths of the airport on a rickety conveyor belt. Toño turns to the right and, seeing no one, turns to the left, and comes face to face with his older brother, Beto.

"It's been a long time, brother!" Beto says with a smile. When Toño last saw him, he resembled the letter T: all skin and bones with a broad mustache across his face. Now, his mustache is gone, and the fleshiness of his cheeks betrays the fact he hasn't missed a meal in quite some time, perhaps years.

Toño wraps his arms around his brother and withdraws in the space of a breath as he remembers the men in his family don't hug. "It has been a long time. It's good to see you again," he says.

They each step back to take a look at what the years apart

have done to the other. Toño could swear Beto is wearing the same navy-blue pants he wore every day before Toño left, his favorite pair. His belt is cinched tight, and the buckle is no longer visible because his belly has gotten large enough to experience the effects of gravity. Wisps of black chest hair stick out from between unclasped buttons on his white polo shirt.

"You've been eating well!" Toño says as he taps his brother's belly.

"Delfina makes sure I eat."

"Delfina?"

"My woman. We live together. We'll get married one of these days but what's the rush, you know?"

Toño nods.

"Don't they feed you in America?" Beto asks, his hand squeezing Toño's bicep.

Toño laughs. It's taken conscious effort on his part to stay the same weight over the years. Whenever he found his pants had gotten tighter, he cut back on the size of his meals or skipped a meal altogether. Plus, saving as much money as possible meant he had to be careful about how much was spent on food. "I eat! But clearly not as well as you!"

Beto laughs. "I'm glad you're home."

Toño pulls his luggage from the conveyor belt. "Is it just you?"

"Dad's in the car," Beto says with a nod towards the exit. "He tries to hide it, but I can tell he's excited to see you."

"Then let's go!"

Jose Angel leans on a dusty white pickup truck, watching the stream of people leaving the airport. They spot each other, and Toño quickens his pace to close the distance between them, leaving Beto a few paces behind. Jose Angel rushes forward to meet his second son. "Here, let me take that from you!" he says, taking Toño's duffel bag from him with one of his large metal hands. He puts it into the bed of the truck before he turns around to take a look at his son.

For a moment the two men stand apart, both of them studying the ways in which the other man has changed. Toño left as a scrawny, uncertain youth and has come back a wiry, confident man.

Jose Angel's bald spot has grown, and Toño can't remember if his father's shoulders have always been this stooped of if the pressure of time has forced them down.

All of a sudden, Toño steps forward and wraps his arms around his father. The tricky nature of time permeates the embrace. While the physical effects of the years are obvious to both men, it's also clear that time was put on pause when Toño left, and now that he's back, the two of them can pick up right where they left off.

"Thanks for letting me come home," Toño says.

"You will always have a home," Jose Angel says, emotion choking his words.

Toño's stomach falls and tears well in his eyes. Before any liquid can fall, Beto tells the two of them to get into the car. "Let's get moving!" he says.

The three men sit shoulder to shoulder in the cab of the truck. Beto drives, Toño sits in the passenger seat, and Jose Angel, the smallest of the three men, sits between them. During the drive, Beto asks Toño about his time in America but always finds a way to hijack the conversation to tell Toño about what he's been doing in El Salvador. Toño doesn't mind; this is the relationship he and his brother have had their entire lives. Beto craves the spotlight. He has no problem sharing personal details, while Toño tends to shy away from letting the world know more about himself than is necessary. When Toño does speak, he finds it hard to articulate the ways in which he spent the years. His life in America seems commonplace, the natural progression an immigrant would take if they wanted to make as much money as possible in the shortest amount of time. He doesn't want to talk about the women who decided he wasn't worth their future.

Toño finds out Beto makes enough money selling cars in San Salvador to afford a house in Santa Lucia, a town on the other side of the market. "The truck we are riding in will be sold by the end of next week!" Beto says with pride.

"Does your woman work?"

"No, she stays at home. They aren't married," Jose Angel says.

Toño can tell this is, or has been, a point of contention between the two of them.

"When we met, the junta still looked down on the church. I guess we haven't gotten around to making it official," Beto says. "Plus, she's pregnant."

Toño and Jose Angel both stare at the eldest brother, who doesn't take his eyes from the road ahead until the truck has been parked on the street outside the family home in San Ramon. As soon as they arrive, the entire family rushes out to greet Toño. Felicita watches from the doorway as three of Toño's younger siblings surround him, peppering him with questions.

"What's America like?" Alfonso says.

"Do you miss it already?" asks Rosa.

"Why did you come back?" Maria says. She doesn't allow her excitement to show, and hers is the only question Toño answers.

"Because I missed everyone!" Toño says. He wades through his brothers and sisters and gives his mother a hug. Carmen and Lillian stand next to their mother, and he hugs them too.

Lillian, now eight, was two years old when Toño left and has no memory of her brother. Toño kneels on one knee to bring himself face-to-face with her. "I know you probably don't remember me, but I remember you," he says to the youngest member of his family.

Lillian stares at Toño with wide eyes then runs away.

"Give her time. Once she starts talking she doesn't shut up!" Carmen says as Toño stands up. Carmen is the closest in age to Toño, and he is delighted to see the young woman she has become. He wonders if there are any men in his sister's life.

"Come grab this stuff," Jose Angel commands Alfonso.

The women of the house spend the afternoon cooking a welcome-home dinner for Toño while the men—Beto, Toño, and Jose Angel—sit under a banana tree to escape the afternoon heat.

Word spreads through the town that Toño has returned. Male neighbors stop by to say hello and end up seated under the tree to hear what life is like in America. At one point there are over a dozen men listening to Toño describe the subway system in New York City.

As the smells wafting from the kitchen become more distinct, each visitor excuses himself in order to prevent the owner of the house from extending obligatory dinner invitations. Toño catches glimpses of self-stirring pots and misses Lori, wondering if she could ever learn to command the tools of her kitchen the same way his mother does.

Angel is the only member of the family missing at the dinner table. The table's four legs sit on red clay tiles beneath a patio covered only by a roof. Leaves from surrounding trees filter light cast by the setting sun. The surviving rays spill onto the table and highlight the efforts made by the women: mounds of fresh tortillas, three kinds of pupusas, plantains, and rice.

Conversation stops as everyone begins to eat. Alfonso is the last to finish. He is young enough to eat as much as he wants and not gain an ounce of fat. Toño, impressed when his brother throws another set of three tortillas on his plate, asks, "Where does all of this go?"

"I need my fuel!" Alfonso says with his mouth full.

Jose Angel reaches over the food to turn on a single light bulb hanging from a cord above the center of the table, careful he doesn't tap the glass with any of his iron fingers. Felicita stands up and begins to clear the table. With a series of looks, she is able to urge her daughters to help. Rosa emits a loud sigh and drags her feet as she walks around the table collecting dirty dishes. The broom in the corner springs to life and begins to clear the floor of debris.

"Too bad Delfina couldn't make it," Toño says to Beto.

"She didn't want to come to the airport, so I left her at home."

"Guess she didn't want to eat," Jose Angel says.

"Maybe. I'm sure I'll hear about it tonight. Toño, did you leave any women behind in America?"

Toño thinks about Lori, about Paula. "None worth mentioning," he says.

"We will have to find you one here!" Jose Angel exclaims.

CHAPTER THIRTY-SIX

Jose Angel shakes Toño awake before the sun begins to rise. "Get up, we have work to do." He fills a bucket of water to take to the cows.

Toño never expected to be treated like a guest, but he would've appreciated some sort of warning the night before his first day back. He sits up in the hammock, turns to the side, and puts both feet on the ground. Time to earn his keep. "If the old man can wake up this early to get his work done, then I can. I'm still young," Toño says to himself.

A pot of coffee has already been made. Toño pours himself a cup of the steaming liquid and takes his first sips before he goes to the stone room, separate from the house, where the toilet is located. Between the coffee and the chill of the morning, he is wide awake within minutes. Looking out at the land behind the house, he is grateful to be home, grateful to be awake this early, grateful to be able to return to the life of a farmer in El Salvador after leaving behind his life in America.

When the animals have been fed and watered, both men grab a machete and begin their morning walk around the land. The sun begins to rise and witness the father and son walking side by side on the well-worn path out of the trees and into the fields.

"There have been squatters near the sugarcane, I made them leave a few days ago. Let's go make sure they haven't come back," Jose Angel says.

The two men come to a clearing on one of the two farthest corners from the house. Stale evidence of a fire is between two trampled spots on the ground where the squatters must have slept.

Jose Angel inspects the area. "Looks the same as yesterday," he says. He walks to the edge of the clearing and waves Toño over to him. "They took some sugarcane with them when they left."

Short stumps cover an area the size of their patio. "Did you know them?"

"I'd never seen them before."

"Are you going to tell the police?"

"Not worth it for this much. I try and stay away from them as much as possible since they have their hands full with the guerrillas. If I do tell the police about the stolen sugarcane they could think I was helping them."

"Even if you say it was stolen?"

"They could claim I only reported it to keep my name clean. You don't understand how backward things are now, Toño. Nothing is the same. We have to be careful all the time. Neighbors turn on one another, and even though I don't think ours would turn against us, I don't want to take the chance."

Toño gets annoyed at hearing how he doesn't understand the way his country, his home, works. He grew up here, after all! Everything seems the same to him, and he gets the sense his father has created ghosts to scare his son.

They continue on the tour of the outskirts of their land until their path is interrupted by a dirt road. They turn left and walk along the road for a dozen paces before they get to another path on their right, into the grove of coconut trees that had dropped its cargo all around Toño the last time he was there. Nothing seems out of the ordinary, so the pair head back home.

"Tomorrow we can walk through the interior. It won't take so long," Jose Angel says.

They have been walking for over two hours, and Toño has worked up an appetite. Memories of his father's routine trickle back to him. As long as nothing has changed, two days from now they won't walk around their land at all. Instead, they will walk to the market and buy whatever is on the list Felicita will provide. Toño wonders if Angel ever accompanied their father the way Toño did when he was younger and does again now that he has returned. Is Alfonso ever expected to join the inspection of the land? Toño was younger than Alfonso when he started walking with his father. Maybe now that he is back, Alfonso has been let off the hook in order to focus on school. Then again, he was expected to work the farm and go to school.

None of Toño's family are in the house when the two men return. The only person in the house is the young wife of a family Jose Angel lets live in a small shack on his land in exchange for work. She is bent over a bucket of soapy water, washing clothes. Jose Angel doesn't bother with formal introductions. "Tell Sandra what you want to eat and she'll make it."

"I want my eggs," Jose Angel tells her.

"Of course. And for you?" Sandra asks Toño.

"Plantains," Toño replies.

"That's it? So simple!" she says with a laugh.

"Maybe some sausage too," Toño says. "Yes, some sausage."

"Okay, I'll make it right now."

Jose Angel excuses himself to go to the bathroom, and Toño suspects this trip is also engrained in his father's routine. Toño sits down at the table on the patio and compares his life in

America to his life here while he watches Sandra work. Sandra cooks on a stone oven that requires wood to be fed into the fire underneath the range. If Americans had to worry about firewood in order to cook, they would all starve! The lack of walls on the patio will also take some getting used to. In theory, anyone could walk up through their land and into the back of their house. The only thing stopping anyone from doing so is the row of connected houses that extends down their block and turns down the street next to theirs. Any would-be thief would have to go past so many houses just to get to his that the odds are against his house being a target. Plus, there are other families in shacks along the way that anyone with malicious intent would have to pass. After life in America, the lack of security will take some getting used to.

Sandra serves father and son their food—Jose Angel's usual turns out to be eggs with chopped tomatoes—and before she has a chance to return with a glass of water for each of them the food on both plates is gone. Toño's eyes become heavy as the early morning rise takes its toll.

"That was fast! Drink this before you fall asleep," she says.

"I know when to wake up by when I have to piss," Jose Angel says to Toño. "Works every time." He lifts the glass with two stiff hands, and the contents of the glass disappear after one long drink.

Toño laughs at his father's logic but can't fault the man for coming up with a system that works for him. The effectiveness of the natural alarm clock must run in the family, because Toño wakes up forty-five minutes later and rushes to the bathroom. His father is on his way out when Toño gets to the stone building.

"So your alarm works too!" Jose Angel says.

Toño can't believe he hasn't thought of so simple a method before. As a boy, he always wondered how his father knew when to wake up, since no alarm clock was ever heard going off in their small house. He never imagined the tool was something as simple as a large glass of water. One of Toño's old friends comes to the house to visit. His name is Esteban, and he couldn't be more different from the bear back in Maryland who shares the same name. His arms are thin, and he has a small gut. His skin is dark brown and hands are rough from working in the fields. Together, they sit at the table on the patio and reminisce about old times. When Esteban asks Toño about America, Toño tells him the story is best saved for another day. His friend understands and doesn't press the issue. In the following silence, Toño suggests they go to the store and get a drink, his treat.

"Let's go," Esteban says.

Jose Angel is dozing off but must have left an ear open, because as soon as he hears Toño is about to leave, he informs the two friends he will accompany them. "Let me put on my shoes," he says.

Esteban leans in close to Toño when Jose Angel goes into his bedroom. "He follows you around like you were one of his girls," he whispers.

"I know. He's just worried," Toño says.

"How long do you think it will last?"

"Maybe until he realizes I don't care how the country is. This is my home and I'll live how I want."

"That attitude's the reason he follows you around!" Esteban says. "This country belongs to the government and the guerrillas, nobody else. The sooner you realize that, the sooner he will leave you alone to do as you please."

Esteban, Toño, and Jose Angel walk to the small store and, drinks in hand, sit outside in the shade provided by the building. Toño asks Esteban a question that has been on his mind while they sit outside the store. "Do you remember Lucia?"

"Lucia . . . can't say I do," Esteban says.

"She was Sebastian's younger sister."

"Oh yeah! Didn't you used to tease him that you were going to take her out?"

Toño laughs. "He used to get so mad when I would say that! Are they still around?"

"As far as I know. Every so often I will see her at the field watching the Deers."

"Do they have a game here this weekend?"

"I believe so. Are you going to come watch?" Esteban says.

"I think I will," says Toño.

Five young men, all carrying guns, walk by. When Jose Angel sees his son stare at the weapons, he tells his son to look at the ground.

"Guerrillas," his father says once the men have passed.

"So? We can't look at them?"

"Not if you want to stay out of trouble," says Esteban.

Toño can't help but become indignant. "I can look at whatever I want!" He is careful to say this low enough so nobody but the three of them can hear.

"This isn't America, Toño," Esteban warns.

"How many times do I have to tell you that El Salvador is different now?" Jose Angel says. "The killing used to happen at night and the murderers would run away. Now they kill during the day without worrying about what could happen."

Toño wants to press the issue but doesn't want to further upset his father. "Let's go back," he says to Jose Angel. "It was good seeing you, Esteban. Come over again soon."

"Good seeing you too, Toño," Esteban says.

Toño gets up with his father, and together they walk back to the safety of their home.

CHAPTER THIRTY-SEVEN

EVERYONE in the town makes sure their work is done so they can attend the soccer game Saturday afternoon. Toño, Alfonso, and Jose Angel get to the field half an hour before the game is about to start, Alfonso with his cleats and shin guards in hand. People are already gathered around the dusty field. One group of older men has amassed a large pile of empty beer cans. There is a cart selling snow cones. Its owner, a woman nicknamed Azucar, fills a cup with shaved ice from a large block of ice inside her cooler. She sells two flavors: coconut and pineapple. Alfonso asks Jose Angel for ten cents to buy one, and when Jose Angel doesn't give it to him, he turns to Toño.

"Can you give me ten cents?" Alfonso says.

Toño looks at his father above his younger brother and detects a tiny shake of the older man's head. "Sorry, maybe next time."

"Fine, I'll see if someone else will buy me one!" Alfonso says.

"You do that," Toño says as his younger brother rushes away.

While Toño was in America, someone installed three rows

of aluminum stadium seats next to the field. Toño and Jose Angel sit down and watch Alfonso approach the members of the Deers who have already arrived on the far side of the field.

"Should be a good game today," Jose Angel says to Toño while the Deers warm up.

"Who are we playing?"

"The policemen from San Salvador."

"I remember playing them, they were always pretty good."

"Our team is pretty good too, you'll see."

Both teams leave the field a few minutes before kickoff and return walking single file from the direction of the town, Alfonso halfway through the line. They walk to opposite sides of the field and set their bags down. The referees follow, and once they set their gear down near a corner flag, they walk into the middle of the field and gesture for captains from each team to join them. In the center of the field, the men all shake hands before the referee tosses the coin. The home team selects to defend the right side of the field, and the visitors receive the kickoff. The game begins with each team making deliberate passes while they search for openings to be exposed in the opposition's defense. Alfonso is on the sidelines.

Toño keeps one eye on the game and the other on the crowd around the field, looking for Sebastian. His true desire is to find Lucia, but he doubts she would be at the game since everyone around the field is, for the most part, male.

Towards the end of the first half of play, Toño sees a man and a woman approach the field from the direction of the barrios. They get closer and he recognizes Sebastian, and, unless his eyes deceive him, Lucia is with him. They stand behind the policemen on the far side of the field.

The referee blows the whistle to end the first half, and each team goes to their respective side.

"I'll be right back," Toño says. He gets up before his father has the chance to get a word of warning out. After he walks to the far side of the field, he shakes hands with Sebastian and Lucia then sticks his hands in his pockets as the three of them talk. Toño stays on the far side of the field until midway through the second half before he returns to his seat next to his father.

"Who were they?" Jose Angel says.

"Sebastian and Lucia. I went to school with them."

"Where are they from?"

"Sangre Cristo."

After a few moments of silence, Toño informs his father he has made plans to visit Lucia the following night. "She said she isn't married, and she didn't object to me coming to visit, so I assume she doesn't have a man. Sebastian wasn't too happy about it but he'll live, he can't keep her alone forever."

The game is tied 0–0. The last ten minutes of the game turn into a frantic scramble for a goal as both teams press the attack, to the detriment of their defenses. The goalie for the Deers has to make a miraculous save, and Jose Angel leans over to his son to tell him how the national team has shown interest in the young man. "Could you imagine a player from the Deers playing for our country?" The Deers almost score on the far side of the field, but the ball bounces off the upright and goes out of bounds. The fans had all stood up while the ball was in the air, and together they emit a collective groan as they retake their seats. The goalie makes one more save—"Told you he's good!" Jose Angel says—and the referee blows the final whistle. The game ends in a tie without Alfonso seeing the field.

Felicita makes enough food for dinner to feed both her own family and the family who lives on their land. Sandra and her husband, Alejandro, show up showered and dressed with their baby girl in tow.

"Do they come over every week?" Toño asks his sister Maria as she sets the table.

"Every Saturday," she says with contempt.

Toño nods. He doesn't want to deal with her sour mood, so he walks away and ends up talking to Alejandro while Sandra and the baby sit with Lillian and Rosa.

"How long have you lived here?" Toño asks the young man.

"Almost two years now. I've heard a lot about you."

"What did you hear?"

"Just about how you went to America. They say you saw Los Angeles, New York City, and Washington, D.C. I wish I was brave enough to leave before I had her," he says with a motion of his chin to his baby.

"Plenty of people leave their family behind to make money. I did."

"It's different when you're the head of your own family. I don't want to miss out on her growing up."

"That's very responsible of you."

Alejandro grabs a glass of water from the table next to him and takes a drink. "Weren't you scared?"

"Scared of what?"

"Scared to go to America! To leave your home behind."

"Well my father said I could always come back, so what was there for me to worry about? It was always my plan to come back once I made enough money to set myself up back here."

"That's nice of him. I wish I had a father like that." Alejandro tells Toño how he grew up in one of the barrios with a drunken father who would disappear for weeks at a time. "The last time he left he never came back."

"Have you ever seen him again?"

"No, he just vanished. I think he got involved with the guerrillas. Maybe he was killed but who knows? This country isn't what it used to be."

Jose Angel is sitting in a chair watching two of his daughters play with the baby. Toño gestures towards the man with his head. "You sound like him," he says to Alejandro.

Alejandro swells like a dry stone submerged in water when he hears the comparison. "What makes you say that?"

"He says the country has gone to shit. Sometimes it seems like he doesn't want me here."

"It has. I think he's just worried about you, that's all. You're used to America, where everything is fair and they have a stable government. Everyone free to do what they want, be who they are. Is is it true there are a lot of blacks?"

Toño chuckles. "Blacks, Asians, whites . . . all the colors we never see here."

"I can't imagine!"

"It took some getting used to, but at the end of the day everyone is the same. We all just wanted to earn money and have our own little slice of life."

"Dinner's ready!" Maria yells even though everyone is well within earshot. Felicita, Maria, and Sandra serve every person their meal. A steaming plate of food is placed in front of Toño: a small piece of steak, salad, rice, and beans. There are two stacks of tortillas on the table for everyone to grab at their leisure. Each plate contains the same foods in the same ratios, the difference being that the men's plates have a higher quantity of food than the women's.

"How come he gets so much more?" Lillian says as she looks at Alfonso's plate.

"He's a growing boy and needs his strength. Now be quiet and eat your food," Jose Angel says to his daughter.

The men sit beneath the banana tree while the women clean up after dinner. The sun goes down, and the insects come out alongside the noise of nocturnal creatures scrambling through the trees. The evening's conversation revolves around soccer, in particular the game earlier that day, and ends when Jose Angel begins to snore.

Felicita hears her husband and comes to lead him to their bed. The young family leaves to return to their shack, and the rest of Toño's family are silent so as not to disturb the patriarch. Toño isn't tired and wishes he knew somewhere to go and spend his Saturday night. He considers taking a walk around the town to see if any of his neighbors are still awake, but his father's words about how the country isn't the same echo in his mind.

Toño lies down in the hammock and waits for sleep to wrap her arms around him as gunshots ring out in the distance.

CHAPTER THIRTY-EIGHT

THE PLAN IS to show up at Lucia's house at six on Sunday night. A visit at that hour comes with the assumption he will be invited to take a seat at her dinner table, but if she hasn't eaten yet, Toño is prepared to walk with her to get food. A few of his neighbors always make enough food to sell, and there should be some people near her who operate the same way.

Toño begins to get ready at five. He washes his face and combs his hair before his customary two sprays of cologne in the center of his chest. At five thirty, with a fresh shirt and khaki pants on, he informs his parents he is going to Sangre Cristo. "I should be back later tonight," he says.

Jose Angel walks out from the bedroom, buttoning his shirt as he walks. "I'm coming with you."

Toño blinks twice. Esteban's assessment rings out between his ears: He treats you like one of his girls. "You know I'm going to visit a woman, right?"

"So? I don't want you walking around alone."

"I'll be fine!"

"You don't know how it is here, Toño."

"You keep saying that," Toño says through clenched teeth.

He has to use every ounce of his power to keep from losing his temper. He reminds himself of all his father has done for him and remembers how his father said he could always come home. Toño never thought this could be what his father meant.

"And I will until you get it through your head! Part of me wishes you never have to see the country the way I see it, but the other part knows your life is in danger until you do."

Toño has half a mind to cancel the visit with Lucia. She will forgive him, after all. She is from the barrio and he is from the town. Any woman in her situation would have no choice but to acquiesce to whatever arrangement someone like Toño proposes, someone who has spent long enough in America to earn the kind of money women like Lucia can only dream of. Toño does his best to force these kinds of thoughts from his mind. He doesn't like to think of anyone as inferior to anyone else. That was the part of America that bothered him most, how other Salvadorans looked down on him because he didn't have his papers. In his mind, people are people, and everyone deserves to be treated with respect. But it's hard for him to ignore the clear class distinction reflecting off the faces of everyone he talks to now that he's returned.

Father and son walk the dirt road to the barrio. Jose Angel tries to make conversation, but Toño's one-word answers make it hard for anything to stick.

Lucia's house sits in the middle of a row of small houses, each so small they can't contain more than one room. Sheets of metal make up each house's roof. Toño hopes the neighbors are cordial with one another since their lives occur in such close proximity. Could they all be related to Lucia and Sebastian? What appears to be communal hammocks are spread out among the available trees. A few thin chickens peck the ground out front, and one brave rooster struts towards Toño and his father to investigate the newcomers.

Both Toño and his father reach down and brush the dust from their pant legs as they stand just outside the piece of metal attached to hinges between a rusty wire fence, which serves as a front gate. Toño imitates the rooster and stands tall, walks through the gate, and approaches the front of the house. The door is thrown open before he can knock.

"Hi, Toño!" Sebastian says. When he sees Jose Angel behind Toño, he bows his head. "Hello, señor," he says to the older man.

"Good to see you again," Toño says with a weak smile.

"Come in, come in," Sebastian says. He steps back and holds the door open for his guests.

Sebastian always seemed upset whenever Toño joked about how he wanted to take Lucia out when they were in high school. His attitude has changed now that he sees Toño is serious. Maybe Lucia had a talk with him, or maybe it was his mother, but either way Toño is convinced a lot of Sebastian's attitude shift has to do with the ways his sister will benefit if Toño chooses to marry her. Toño isn't sure how he feels about the change.

Lucia is seated next to her mother, a wood stove between them. The mother is a tired old woman who is missing all her teeth and whose hair is almost all gray. Toño wonders if Lucia's father is in their lives anymore. If he was, wouldn't he want to be here when his daughter received a male visitor? No way he would have gone out and missed the chance to size up the man who wants to get to know his little girl. Maybe he died, killed by the guerrillas like Alejandro believes his dad might have been, or maybe he ran off with some younger woman.

Introductions are made, and it comes out that Jose Angel and Lucia's mother have known each other from a distance for years.

"Your daughter is very lovely," Toño tells Lucia's mother.

She smiles a toothless smile, and Toño is struck by how the woman accepts her appearance and makes no apologies for the toll taken by time.

The evening's conversation revolves around Toño's time in America. Lucia and Toño are unable to have any form of private discussion with so many people around them. Every time Toño directs a question to the girl, either her mother or her brother answers for her. In her shy smile Toño finds the desire for the two of them to be alone, and in another circumstance or another country, he would have asked if she wanted to take a walk. Here, now, he knows his father will insist on being their chaperone, so he buries the thought.

"So you lived with Manuel for a while?" Sebastian remarks when Toño discusses the beginning of his time in New York.

"For years. Even after he moved out I still saw him. Not as often as before because he was busy with his family, but we would go to church together on Sundays."

Lucia's mother nods and gives Toño a thin-lipped smile of understanding. "It's good that you carve out time to go to church. That's very important." She looks at Lucia and gives the girl a nod of approval.

"Mama can't walk to church anymore," Lucia says in a small voice, the first words she has uttered since the group sat down.

Toño finds himself enchanted by her tone, her inflection, and the space between her words. "That's too bad," he says. As soon as this statement has left his lips he wishes there was something more he could say, some question he could ask, in order to keep her talking. Some secret phrase or password that would open up the treasures hidden behind her sparkling eyes.

Everyone else in the room stays silent and has their eyes on their feet in hopes the girl takes the space to elaborate. She doesn't disappoint. "I read the Bible to her this morning for an hour before we prayed together. Sebastian can't sit still long enough to listen to me read, but he joined us in prayer."

Toño is convinced this is the type of religiosity his own mother would display if she were placed in a similar situation. In two small phrases, Lucia has been able to prove herself a woman Toño would be proud to start a family with.

The rest of the visit is spent trying to get Lucia to talk about herself, but the girl always finds a way to bring the conversation back to her mother and her brother. Before Toño and his father leave, he tells Lucia and her family he will come back next Sunday.

"That girl cares a lot about her family," Jose Angel says to Toño on their walk back home. The bottom of the sun has disappeared below the horizon, and nocturnal insects buzz in the trees on each side of the road.

Toño nods. Individual lights outside the homes of San Ramon cut into the night. Toño watches as insects fly into one glass bulb over and over again, confused by the presence of the artificial sun when the rest of their world has begun to grow dark.

CHAPTER THIRTY-NINE

THE PATH to Tio Abel's house takes Toño and his father through the heart of San Ramon in the sweltering heat of midday. They pass the elementary school and its fresh coat of mint-green paint.

"Looks good. Much better than I remember," Toño says in an offhand way.

Jose Angel straightens despite the weight of the sun and puffs out his chest. "You paid for that," he says.

Toño looks at his father, confused. "What do you mean?"

"The guerrillas vandalized the school, painted their slogan on every wall. We asked the government to repaint the school, we didn't want people to think this town was pro-guerrilla, but we couldn't get anyone from the capital to listen to us. The church said they wanted to raise the money and your mother thought we should donate to the cause. I ran into Father Cristobal after the school was painted and he thanked me for our donation, said almost all of the money came from us. Came from you."

"I sent that money for you, not for the school."

"You sent that money for me and I decided it was best to help out the community. You should be proud!"

Toño takes another look at the school, at its bright green doors. There's no evidence to suggest it's ever been vandalized.

"It does look good."

"Nobody else knows it was us, or you, if that makes you feel any better."

"It does." He doesn't want the rest of the town to know about how much money he's sent over the years or how much money he has with him now. Every time someone needed money they would come to ask for handouts, and Toño doesn't want to get in the habit of giving his money to anyone other than his family. It would just cause more problems, and people already treat him like he's changed.

Outside the town, the two men walk past the dusty soccer field. "Does Alfonso ever play in the games?" Toño asks.

"Only if his team is ahead by a few goals. He's still young, but they tell me he is a fearless defender," Jose Angel says.

Toño remembers what it was like being on the field with his team and wishes he had played more often, or at all, when he was in America. Whatever skills he had possessed have evaporated after so long, but he hopes he can practice with the team soon, even if it's just to get some exercise.

They get to Toño's uncle's house, his mother's brother, after a twenty-minute walk past the field. The shack sits right on the dirt road, and there is a small clearing behind the structure where straight rows of plants emerge from the soil. Weeds have taken root between the rows, and Toño wonders how long it has been since his uncle has taken the time to fight back their inevitable onslaught.

Jose Angel knocks on the door. "Abel! You in there?"

Tio Abel opens the door. Black-and-gray whiskers combine with the lines on his face to give the impression he is much older than he is. His greasy hair is parted to the left and his eyes are red. He takes one look at Toño and goes in for a hug.

"Welcome home, Toño!" he says. The man reeks of alcohol.

"Good to see you again, uncle."

Tio Abel holds the door open for the two men once he releases Toño. "Come in, come in. Do either of you want something to drink?"

Jose Angel holds up his hand. "No thanks, I'm good."

"Toño?"

The son mimics his father's hand gesture. "No thanks."

The shack is one small room. There is a curtain that divides the space in two. The curtain isn't drawn shut, and the foot of a bed pokes out. A dirty pot is on the stove, and next to it is one plate. On the plate is one cup with one fork and one knife inside. The space reeks of alcohol, sweat, and claustrophobia.

Abel pulls two chairs from against the wall and tells his guests to sit down. He sits on the foot of his bed with a smile on his face.

Jose Angel looks around the room and crinkles his nose. "How long has it been since you've cleaned up?"

"A few days, I think. Could be a week," Abel says with a dash of pride.

Jose Angel's nostrils flare. "Let's take the chairs out back," he says.

Toño and his father each grab a chair and walk out the back door. Abel follows with a guitar in his hand. He grabs a bucket, flips it over, sits down, and begins to tune the instrument.

They spend the early afternoon talking, most of their conversation revolving around Toño's time in America. Abel strums his guitar in rhythm with their conversation. Bright, cheerful notes ring out when Toño describes his adventure from Los Angeles to New York City, and slow, sorrowful music accompanies Toño's description of Manuel moving out of the apartment. The sad music inspires Toño to talk about Paula, about how she wouldn't fly away from her husband, one of the few times in the rest of his life Toño will talk about the woman with wings.

Jose Angel walks forward, squats down, and begins to pick weeds from between the rows of plants closest to the men while Toño continues his tale.

The music comes to a crescendo when Toño meets Lori and enters a minor key upon his return home. Even though Toño tells his story as facts, the guitar detects the underlying current without elaboration from its protagonist.

"You shouldn't have come back," Abel says.

Before he is able to register what's happening, Toño finds himself picking weeds as well, lost in the steady strum of the guitar. Sweat colors the shirts of both men as their circle of work extends out like ripples on a pond. Abel is considerate enough to play the guitar louder and louder as the men get farther away. He sings a sad song about lost love at the top of his lungs when the two men are on the far side of the clearing.

Toño stands up after the last weed is picked. His fingers bleed, and sweat has matted his hair to his head. When he looks back at Abel, the old man smiles and stops playing. In the midst of his song he has grabbed a bottle of liquor and, as Jose Angel and Toño watch, he turns the bottle over to show it's empty. The specters of the men, women, and children who came to stand on the living side of death to hear the music all turn back into the void now that the music has stopped.

"You did it again!" Jose Angel says in mock anger.

"Did what?" a drunk Abel slurs.

"Enchanted us with your music! Is this why you wanted us to come over? Because you knew your garden needed tending to?"

"You suggested we sit out back, remember? Besides, the

guitar chooses the music, not me. I'm just a drunk! The instrument knows just what to say to pull the truth from you, or in this case, to pull the weeds from the ground."

Toño is surprised his uncle can string together so many words. He wipes his dirty hands on his pants and walks back to his seat, exhausted. His legs have regained feeling and scream at him for subjecting them to a squat for so long. "How about that drink?" he says.

Jose Angel sits down as well, and when asked if he wants a drink too, he says he's fine, that he just needs to rest.

The host stumbles on his way inside and returns with two beers. He pops the top off both and hands one to Toño as he takes a long drink from the other.

All three men have run out of words. Jose Angel motions to Toño with his head that it's time for them to leave.

"Let's get back. Your mother should have dinner ready soon."

"He still has some of his beer left!" Abel says.

"He can drink it while we walk."

They say goodbye and leave Abel to his drunkenness. Toño, once he finishes the beer, tosses the bottle on the ground and is amazed at how refreshed he feels. His fingers have stopped bleeding, and the sweat around his collar has disappeared. If it wasn't for the dirt on the ground and beneath his fingernails, there would be no indication he just spent the past few hours digging up the past.

Jose Angel is annoyed and covered with sweat. "You left a woman behind in America?"

Toño, startled by his father's sudden question, doesn't respond.

"Well?"

"She refused to come back with me."

"As she should have! This country is no place for either of you."

"This is my home," Toño says, the strength of his voice failing him.

"This was your home. And you left. For good reason, but you left. Now, you had the potential for another home in America, with an American woman, and you left that behind too. When will you learn there's nothing for you here but to die on the land?"

Their conversation continues with Felicita after dinner, once the rest of the family has gone off to kill the time before bed.

"If I don't belong here, where do I belong?" Toño says to his parents, the first words he's uttered since he walked through the front door. He's seated at the dinner table with Jose Angel while Felicita cleans the kitchen.

"You know where you belong. What's your plan now that you're back?" Jose Angel asks. "You have money. You want a farm. You think this will attract a woman? It might, but your thinking is flawed. You have it reversed. First you find a woman, then create a life. Together. You found a woman and you left her behind."

Felicita stands over Jose Angel and lays a hand on his shoulder.

Jose Angel exhales. "I'm going to the bathroom," he says.

"I want you to think about something, Toño," she says in a soft voice, the two of them now alone. "Men think women are like tools, something they acquire. Even your father thinks like this. Women know how to make the tools work for them. It's the same in relationships. You must play your part."

"And what's my part?"

"To provide."

"I'm trying to do that! Once I have my farm I'll have no problem providing."

"How can I explain what I mean . . ." She looks around the room and spots the broom sweeping the floors. Felicita grabs the stick and holds it still. "See this broom? It could sweep all day long, but it has no idea what needs to be cleaned, not until I tell it where to go. What good does that do?"

Toño shakes his head.

Felicita points out past the back of the patio to their land in the distance. "Right now you are sweeping outside, far away from home. You're not playing your part! But if you learn to listen you'll stop wasting your time cleaning the dirt."

CHAPTER FORTY

ALFONSO WAKES the house up in the middle of a Sunday night after Toño has been home for two and a half months. The whole town will soon find out the news Toño's brother has rushed home to share. Toño stays in the hammock and listens as his younger brother, still breathless from his run home, tells his father what has happened.

"I was walking back and saw six trucks, all driven by the police, race through town," Alfonso says. He grabs a glass and pours himself water from a pitcher left on the table from the night before. He takes a deep breath and continues. "I watched them pass and followed them to see if they stopped in the town or were just passing through. They pulled into the soccer field— drove right through the middle!—and I walked up to them, asked what was going on, and they told me to go home. Of course I didn't listen . . ."

"Of course," says Jose Angel.

"I snuck around to the far end of the field and saw three dead policemen!"

Toño sits up in the hammock.

"The others were spitting mad. They cursed the guerrillas

217

and said they would burn the town down to smoke out whoever did it. I made sure to stay out of their way so I wouldn't get in trouble, but I think one of them saw me."

Alfonso doesn't seem to be scared at all; rather, he seems excited. Toño tries to remember what it was like to be fourteen and if, at that age, he would have reacted in the same way. Even now, in his early twenties, he doesn't feel any fear, just a trust his father will take care of everything.

Jose Angel looks at Toño, a grave expression on his face. "We were at the field just yesterday to watch the game. I told you this country has gone to shit," he says through a haze of sadness.

More information comes out in the light of the morning. There weren't three bodies, there were four, all of them policemen. They had been abducted in San Salvador, forty minutes away, and murdered somewhere else before their bodies were dumped in San Ramon.

Felicita dictates her grocery list to Toño before he and his father go to the market. She tells her son to grab beans, rice, flour, and two kinds of squash, if anyone has it. Jose Angel is out taking care of the animals, but when he returns they begin the hour-long walk. Accompanying them is Elsa, the neighbor who sells tamales. It's been a few years since she's made the trip on her own; her last solo trip was before the violence in the country began to spill into the daylight from behind the cover of night.

Toño finds himself telling the story of his time in America yet again. He embellishes the parts of the story his father has heard before so the retelling can expose more of the underlying details for the old man. They get to the market just as Toño arrives in Maryland in his story. "Remember where I left off and I'll finish on the way back," Toño tells Elsa as she excuses herself to find customers for her tamales.

Toño and Jose Angel visit vendors who sell each item on

their list. They could split up, but Jose Angel wants to purchase each item himself because, as he says, "business should be taken care of face-to-face." They stop in front of a stand selling sausages.

"Hello, Augusto!" Jose Angel says.

"Hello, señor!" the man behind the counter replies.

The two men exchange pleasantries about the weather before they each lament the state their country is in.

"Hungry?" Augusto asks at a break in the conversation.

"I am. Make it two today."

Toño can't remember his father ever purchasing anything not on the list when they used to come to the market together before he left for America. There was never enough money to justify anything extra. Now, having been sent money for so long, the sausage transaction seems to be a regular occurrence. Toño hopes Angel is able to send enough money that his father can continue to get a sausage every time if he wants. A small treat most people across the border take for granted. Toño remembers how he and Manuel would go to McDonald's, or Burger King, or White Castle, on their trips into Manhattan. He wonders if his friend is still able to afford these little trips now that he has a daughter.

The sausage is served on a sharpened stick. Toño bites into the meat, juice trickles down his chin, and he sticks his head forward to let the liquid drip onto the ground instead of on his shirt. The spice is just right, and the meat is fresh. Toño understands why his father gets one whenever he comes to the market.

Toño and Jose Angel find everything on the list, and Toño slings the sack of food over his shoulder. The two men sit on the edge of a stone fountain at the corner of the market to wait for Elsa. Trash fills the space where water once flowed. Toño remembers when cold water trickled from the fountain, water he was warned to never drink. The two men watch the people in the market and remark on some of the women, Jose Angel appreciating the beauty of the female figure and Toño searching for a potential future.

Elsa returns with an empty sack and a noticeable bulge in her pocket, the reason she wants male company on her trip to and from their town. This much cash on a woman alone is an invitation for an attack. The government can't be relied on to help, and the guerrillas could make her life miserable. But, with a man or two, she can walk without fear of losing the fruits of her labor.

Toño continues to tell the story of his time in Maryland. He tells Elsa about Braddock Heights, about the McDonald's he frequented with Angel on their days off, and about Lori.

Elsa hangs onto every word, her appreciation of romance evident. "Why didn't you stay?" she demands to know.

"She said she would never follow me here, so I had to leave alone. It's always been my dream to come home and have a farm."

Jose Angel shakes his head.

"You're an idiot, Toño," Elsa says. The neighbors have arrived back on their street and see a police car parked on the corner of the block.

Toño laughs. "Why?"

"You threw away the love of a good woman!" She shakes her head, thanks the men for allowing her to join them, and goes inside her home.

Jose Angel motions with his lips to the police car. "Things aren't the same here anymore," he says before they walk into their home and are greeted by two policemen, one older and dark-skinned, one younger and sporting a mustache, sitting at the table with Felicita.

CHAPTER FORTY-ONE

"Juan Antonio?"

"That's me."

"What do you know about the murdered police officers who were discovered at the soccer field this morning?"

Over the next hour, the officers grill Toño about his time in America, his time back in El Salvador, and his whereabouts the night before. After the officers ask how much money he made in America, it becomes clear the men are looking for a bribe. In fact, they may have been looking for a reason to get a substantial bribe from Toño since he came back, but this has been their first opportunity.

"Can I talk to my son alone?" Jose Angel says.

"Of course. We'll be right here," the older officer says with a smile towards Felicita.

Jose Angel tells Toño to offer them money when the two of them are behind the house. "It's the only way out of this. Trust me."

"But I didn't do anything!"

Jose Angel puts a finger to his lips. "Keep it down. It doesn't matter if you did or not, they can make the charges stick. How much money do you have? I'll offer it to them and let's hope it's enough."

Toño tells his father he has over seven thousand in cash.

"Would some weight in your pockets help this go away?" Jose Angel asks the officers when he walks back into the room.

"Depends how heavy you can make them," the older officer says. The younger officer flexes his jaw.

"Three thousand," Jose Angel offers.

"Ten."

"Six."

"Eight."

"Seven, no less."

Jose Angel agrees to seven and Toño feels sick to his stomach.

Toño retrieves the cash from the sock he keeps it in and it's handed over to the younger officer to count. The older officer's nostrils flare, and he must smell blood, because with a wicked smile he asks Jose Angel if he's seen a young man who happened to be at the field the night before. "We heard he lives here."

"We've already paid you," Jose Angel says, his eyes flashing anger.

"You have. That's enough to get us to leave, for now. But if someone else comes looking for the one from the field . . . we need to make sure the rest of the men forget too."

Jose Angel sighs. "How much?"

"Ten thousand."

"Ten thousand! Where do you expect us to get so much money?"

"You don't have to give it to us now. Call the seven a down payment."

"Ten thousand more will make this go away?"

"That's right."

Jose Angel nods and goes into the field. A tense fifteen minutes passes before he returns with a wad of cash in hand. "Here. Ten thousand more. Now will you leave us alone?"

"Of course!" the older officer says while the younger man counts the money, his mustache twitching as the numbers are said under his breath.

Toño asks where the money came from when the officers leave.

"It's from you. I've saved as much as I could to help you buy your farm. It was going to be a surprise."

"Was that all of it?"

Jose Angel pulls a thousand from his pocket and holds it out for Toño. "This is all that's left. Take it."

Toño's refusal lights a fire behind his father's eyes. "If it wasn't for us, you wouldn't have come back," Jose Angel says. "Take it and go back to America. I'm begging you. This country is no place for you."

Toño takes the cash and puts it back in his hiding place, the sock having much more slack in it than before. He calls Angel and has his younger brother send the ten thousand dollars he's stashed in the States.

"I'll do it tomorrow," Angel says without question.

After discussing Toño's life in El Salvador— the situation with the officers is still too fresh for Toño to talk about—Angel tells Toño how mechanical Lori has become.

"She's not doing well. It's like she's rusty. All her movements are slow and there's . . . how do I describe it? It's like she's just going through the motions. But rusty and stiff. She tries to pretend she doesn't care, but Arminda says seeing me reminds her of you."

For the first time, Toño second-guesses his decision and wishes he could see the woman he left behind. Instead of sharing his feelings, he tells Angel he has to go and thanks him for sending the money.

The rest of the week passes by in a haze—his body visits Lucia on Thursday but his mind isn't there—and before Toño knows it he is being woken up on Sunday morning by pots and pans clanging together a few too many times to be a coincidence. Felicita wants the family to wake up and get ready for church. Toño gets the hint and pulls himself from the hammock, appreciative of the fact that at least this aspect of his life is consistent.

"Good morning! Do you want some breakfast?" his mother says.

"Not a lot, I'm still full from last night." His dinner the night before wasn't anything more than he's used to, but the heat of the country makes eating a chore.

While his mother prepares breakfast, Toño walks to the pump and gets enough water to drown his thirst. Three full glasses disappear, and he saves the fourth to drink with his meal. Felicita tells him to wake his siblings when he gets back to the patio. "Everyone except your father," she says.

Toño chuckles. His father is notorious for never going to church even though he makes sure his children go every Sunday. Toño makes the rounds and discovers Alfonso is missing.

Felicita has her back turned to Toño as she labors over the stove. Toño walks up behind her and places a hand on her shoulder. "You know Alfonso isn't here, right?"

"He never is. That boy disappears faster than a plate of sweets around children. Don't worry, he'll meet us at the church."

The mother knows what she is talking about. When the rest of the family take their seats in a pew, they make sure to save a seat for Alfonso. He shows just before mass begins, showered and dressed.

Toño leans across Rosa to talk to Alfonso. "Where did you take a shower?" Toño asks.

"There are lots of showers in town! You just have to know where to look," Alfonso says with a wink.

Felicita grabs Toño's arm, shushes him, and points to the altar, where the priest has taken his place behind the pulpit. Toño tries to pay attention to what the old man says, but after the first few minutes the words become noise. Years of attending services have taught him patience, and he draws upon his deepest reserves of the substance in order to wait for the end of the day's sermon. The heat combined with the slow drawl of the old man causes every pair of eyelids in the church to settle just above closed. The worshippers seem to come alive once the final benediction has been uttered, and Toño remembers his old belief that the freedom after worship is where humans are able to experience God's grace.

On the way out of church, Toño spots Hortensia. It's been a long time since they've seen each other, and Toño almost doesn't recognize her without the red lips and nails he remembers. She's gained weight and leads two young children down the front steps and away from the town.

Toño tries to determine the age of the children and wonders if she was in fact pregnant when he left for America. Felicita must have heard her son performing mental arithmetic, because she leans in close and informs him the baby was born dead.

A wave of relief, followed by guilt, washes over Toño. The conflicting emotions take a few minutes to settle into a cold indifference punctuated by the memory of Hortensia and her ex on the Ferris wheel. He convinces himself he can't even be sure the baby would have been his, so why should he feel relieved, or guilty, about a nonexistent child?

CHAPTER FORTY-TWO

BETO AND DELFINA arrive at the family home Sunday night for dinner. A pregnant Delfina sits in the saddle of a horse and Beto walks alongside, holding the lead.

"He's new, isn't he?" Jose Angel asks while running a hand along the horse's back.

"Why didn't you take one of the cars?" Toño asks.

Beto helps Delfina down from the saddle. "I wanted to give you your welcome home present! I just picked him up," he says to Toño.

"Mine?"

"Yours!"

"You got me a horse?" Toño says, his mouth open in disbelief.

"I never forgot how you sold me half the horse for cheap. Car sales have been steady and I've been able to save enough money to get you this. Now that you're a farmer, I figure you could use one. Much more useful than a car."

"This is too much," Toño says.

"It's nothing," Beto says with a smile. "What's for dinner?"

Delfina helps the rest of the women serve plates piled high

with chicken, rice, and beans to the men before the women sit down at the table with their own plates. Everyone digs in and listens as the younger children talk about what they are learning in school.

"Remember that time we took the animals through the field?" Toño asks Beto during a lull in the conversation.

Beto looks at the ceiling, searching his memory. "Not really. What happened?"

Toño points to Jose Angel. "He told us to take the animals through the streets. You said, 'This way is faster,' pointing through the fields. I said no, but you insisted. We went through the middle of the crops—I think it was beans and corn—and the animals ate their way across!"

Beto's memory stirs. "You said, 'Look what they're doing!' and I told you not to worry!" he says with a laugh.

"And you told the animals to hurry up! We both got beat good for that one." Toño looks at his father. "Do you remember?"

"No, but it sounds like you deserved it! If I told you to go through the road, you should have gone through the road," Jose Angel says.

"You knew it was Beto's fault, you beat him until he was limp on the floor before you turned to me. I can't believe you don't remember!"

Everyone around the table laughs with the three men and their memory.

"They will never know," Beto says. He looks at the younger children, in particular Alfonso.

Alfonso smiles a mischievous smile. "It's your fault you got caught!"

"The neighbors told on us! I think that's why he was so mad," says Toño.

"If it had been our land I don't think I would have even told you to take the road . . . he wouldn't have listened!" Jose Angel says with a nod to Beto, still unable to remember.

Everyone leans back in their chairs after they have eaten their fill. The younger children are restless and ask to be excused. Beto, Toño, and Jose Angel step outside while the women clean up so Toño can take his new horse for a walk down the street.

"Climb on and see how you like him!" Beto says.

Toño takes the horse up and down the block. A chant, familiar to both brothers in their youth, creeps into his mind. "Beto and Toño, Toño and Beto . . ." he says to himself in time with the clack-clack-clack of hooves against stone.

"This is too much," Toño says again when he climbs back down. "What does Delfina say?"

"Nothing. I make the money, not her."

"She's carrying your child," Jose Angel says, disapproval in his voice.

"Will you marry her?" Toño asks.

"In time. What's the rush?" Beto climbs onto the back of the horse.

Jose Angel holds the lead and doesn't let the horse and rider walk away. "The rush is that you have a kid on the way."

"Why don't you bring her into the family?" Toño says.

"Why did you leave your woman in America?" Beto counters.

"She didn't want to come to El Salvador."

"So she doesn't play by your rules and you leave her behind?"

"This isn't about me."

"Delfina plays by my rules without me marrying her. Why should I change anything? I already have what I want."

"You should marry her because it's the right thing to do! For her and for the child," Toño says, louder than intended.

Jose Angel shakes his head and releases the lead, but Beto doesn't move. He glares at Toño from atop the horse.

"You might not want to, but you need to make sacrifices . . . it's what a relationship is all about," Jose Angel says.

"She says the same thing," replies Beto without taking his gaze from his brother.

"Then listen to her!" Toño says.

"Like you listened to Lori?"

It's Toño's turn to glare.

Beto climbs down from the horse. "Maybe El Salvador isn't where you should be," he says.

"Let me worry about that."

Beto ties the horse to the post outside the front door. "All right, if it's such a big deal to you two, let me go tell everyone the news." He walks through the front door, asks the women to stop cleaning, and announces he and Delfina are getting married.

Bright smiles from everyone except Toño light up the room. All Toño can think about is Lori, wondering if he's made a mistake and about how rusty Angel said she's become.

"This is wonderful!" Felicita says with tears in her eyes as she hugs a shocked Delfina.

Beto walks across the room and gives Delfina a hug, pulling her from her catatonic state.

Jose Angel, Beto, and Toño celebrate the announcement with a beer. The women make initial wedding plans while they finish cleaning.

"It's getting late, we should head home," Beto says after draining his bottle.

Delfina agrees. "My feet are swollen. Good thing we have that horse! I wish we'd brought a car though."

"You don't mind if we take the horse, do you, Toño?" Beto says. "I had planned on walking back but her feet won't let her.

We can bring it back another day, or you can come get it. I wanted to surprise you with it and not just tell you about it."

Toño tells his brother it's fine, of course he can take the horse, all the while still thinking about Lori. After the incident with the police officers and tonight's events, he's decided to go back to America but doesn't want to spoil the mood of the evening by telling everyone.

Toño walks outside with the engaged couple and pets his horse, the horse he won't own for much longer. The horse must sense his sadness because tears form in his equine eyes.

Beto helps Delfina onto the horse and they walk away. "Beto and Toño, Toño and Beto . . ." rings out until the horse has turned the corner.

Tears from the horse's eyes drip onto the ground and dot the way back to Beto's house. No amount of rain is able to wash away the dotted trail along the path Beto took back home that evening, and it's only years later, after the stone is replaced with asphalt, that the line between the two houses is broken.

CHAPTER FORTY-THREE

"MAKE SURE YOU WATER THE ANIMALS," Jose Angel reminds Toño before the sun has come up on Monday morning.

Toño nods in the darkness; he doesn't mind when his father issues these reminders and the task has already been placed on his list. He finds himself second-guessing his plan to return to America after a dreamless sleep. Is he willing to give up this stable existence, this comfortable monotony, for the rest of his life?

The way he sees it, he has two possible options. The first would find him with Lucia on a farm in or near his hometown, settled into the rest of his life. The second possibility, terrifying in its reliance on another's soul, finds him sacrificing all he's worked for to return to America and to Lori.

If he does go back, what will his future hold? What is his plan? He won't have any money left. Will Lori agree to take him back penniless?

If so, she'll have to help him get his papers. That's a requirement; he's tired of people looking down on him because he's illegal.

Stay in El Salvador and marry Lucia or move back and hope Lori forgives him? Where does his future family exist?

Toño decides there is no place for him in El Salvador while he pumps water for the animals, alone, without his father watching him like he is one of his daughters. The problem Toño now has to figure out is how to tell everyone his plan without looking like he has given up on El Salvador, and by extension, his family.

Toño leaves to visit Tio Abel, to discuss his decision and hear his uncle's opinion, once the morning's chores have been completed. He gets a block away from his house before Jose Angel comes running behind him, saying he will go visit too. Toño stops at the store to buy some beer for his uncle before he and his father walk past the soccer field where the dead officers were found over a week before.

"What a nice surprise!" Abel says when he opens the door, sees the two men, and sees the beer in Toño's hands. His eyelids cover most of his red eyes, and he walks with slow, deliberate steps into the house. Jose Angel follows Abel inside, and Toño shuts the door behind them.

"Here you go, uncle," Toño says as he hands over the beer.

"Thanks, set it on the floor next to the bed," Abel says.

"We aren't going to stay long. I just wanted to ask your opinion about something," Toño says.

Jose Angel looks at Toño, incredulous. "We came all this way for his opinion?" he says.

"Yes." Toño looks at Abel. "What would you say if I told you I wanted to go back?"

"Back where?" Abel says, cracking the lid on a beer.

"To America."

Jose Angel stares at his son.

"I'd say why not? You already know what's here. Might as well hope for better up there!"

"I've already told you to go back," Jose Angel says under his breath.

"I didn't ask you to come with me," Toño says to his father. "I wanted to hear what he thought."

"Fuck it!" Abel says before he takes a long drink of warm beer.

Toño and Jose Angel leave Abel to drink his calories in peace. As they walk past the soccer field, Jose Angel talks about what a deplorable situation the country finds itself in, sandwiched between the guerrillas and the government. "Don't they see they are tearing us apart?"

After Toño tells the rest of his family his plan—none of whom are surprised—he buys two plane tickets: one to take him to Mexico City and another to take him to Tijuana. Through a chain of townspeople—the first link being his friend Esteban—he is able to contact a pollero who can take him across the border in Tijuana for a third time. Esteban must have told the pollero about Toño's time spent in America, because the crossing will cost twice as much as before.

He calls Angel after his itinerary has been determined. The phone rings and rings but nobody picks up. Toño looks at the clock. If Angel is working at the restaurant tonight, he won't be home for another three hours. Toño calls back when Angel should be getting home from work, and his brother picks up on the third ring.

"Angel? It's me, Toño."

"I know, I could tell right away. Plus, nobody else would call me this late."

"How's McDonald's?"

"You mean how's Lori? Still sad."

Angel then tells Toño how tired he is of living in Braddock Heights. "There are no other Spanish people up here," he says.

"You can practice your English," Toño says.

"Only because I have to! And there aren't any other young people up here. Arminda tries to introduce me to her friends, but the women complain because I don't have papers. How can I have papers? I just got here!"

"They're all like that in America," Toño says. "If you can find a woman who doesn't care about such a small thing, make sure you hang on to her!" He tells Angel he's decided to hang on to Lori and will be coming back next week.

"It'll be good to have you back! How's everything there?"

"A lot has changed since I left," Toño says before telling Angel about using the money he brought to bribe the police officers.

"Why do you think I wanted to come over here?" Angel says.

"I never thought about it. Beto doesn't seem to mind."

"Beto likes to pretend he doesn't notice but he does. He's just stubborn."

"Dad made sure I noticed."

"What do you mean?"

"He doesn't stop talking about how different the country is! And he follows me around everywhere."

Toño tells Angel he will get a ticket to D.C. when he gets to San Diego and will need to get picked up at the airport.

"Just let me know so I can take off work," Angel says.

Toño hangs up the phone and calls Beto's house. Delfina answers and Toño leaves a message for Beto to call him back.

Toño goes to mass with his family for the last time the day before he is scheduled to leave. Lucia shows up with her mother, wearing her best dress. It's obvious she's taken the time arranging her hair. Her mother shuffles by her side, clinging to her arm, in her worn-out housecoat. The two of them walk by Felicita and her brood of children and take a seat on the opposite side of the church.

The day's sermon is about the parable of the prodigal son. The priest talks about the celebration the father in the story throws when the lost son returns and how the father's second son doesn't understand. Toño can't help but be grateful to Beto for not harboring any negative feelings, at least as far as he's aware.

Toño wonders how the father in the story would react if the son decided to leave again. Would he be beyond forgiveness?

This is the first time Toño's ears hear the priest's words and his heart is able to listen. Felicita would be proud.

In Toño's case, the father sent his son away. That has to count for something, doesn't it?

Toño walks right past Lucia on his way out of mass, deep in thought, and is pulled back into the church when he hears her mother whisper, "Everything will be all right. God has a plan for you." He turns around when he gets to the front door and sees Lucia's shoulders shake from silent sobs.

When Beto still hasn't returned his phone call on Sunday night, Toño tries to call again. He asks Delfina to tell Beto he is going back to America the next morning and will call from his home in Maryland.

The morning he is slated to leave, Toño has his life in his backpack over his shoulder and says goodbye to his family. His plan is to walk to the market and catch the bus, which runs from the market to the airport. He walks out the front door and is greeted by a smiling Beto in a red mustang.

"Get in, I'm driving you to the airport!" the older brother says.

Toño looks at his family in the doorway of their home and can tell from his father's smile this was the plan all along.

CHAPTER FORTY-FOUR

Toño GETS on a small plane bound for Tijuana after a brief layover in Mexico City. There is a strange sense of pride in his chest about how his entire life fits into the same backpack he used all those years ago. The clouds roll by during takeoff, and his mind races with thoughts of crossing the border for a third time. His other crossings felt like grand adventures, but now that he's crossing in order to begin the rest of his life in America, there is much more weight than before, and he's worried the pilot hasn't accounted for the extra cargo.

In Tijuana, a cab takes Toño to a garage full of cars in various stages of repair where the pollero has told him they will meet. A young man, not much older than Toño, comes from underneath an old pickup truck and wipes his hands on an oily rag. Black smudges cover his face and arms.

"Carlos," the mechanic says, extending an arm.

Toño shakes the outstretched hand. "Toño," he says. The sharp smell of sweat reaches Toño's nostrils. How long has it been since the mechanic last took a shower?

"Looking to cross, right?"

"I am."

"We leave tonight. Make sure you're back here by ten." Carlos dives back underneath the truck. Toño stands still, not sure what to do with the free afternoon.

"There's a bar two doors down. Decent food. Go hang out in there," the mechanic says from beneath the truck, an arm poking out from the side gesturing to Toño's right.

Toño spends the afternoon watching reruns of Mexican League soccer games from the previous weekend. For dinner he orders chicken and rice.

"My wife makes it fresh every day. You'll like it," the bartender says.

"I do enjoy a home-cooked meal," Toño says to fill the silence.

"Try the coconut flan when you're done, it's her specialty."

Toño takes his time eating dinner and washes it down with a second beer. The bartender seems to know Toño is settled in for the long haul, so he doesn't pressure his patron to order dessert right away. The bartender's patience is rewarded an hour later, and he brings the flan out on a chipped square plate. It disappears in four large bites.

"Good, right?" the bartender says when he clears the plate.

Toño nods, his mouth full.

The bartender smiles. "Told you."

At the start of the third game, Toño takes a look outside and notices the sun is beginning to set. It's almost time to leave. He keeps one eye on the clock and one on the television for the last fifteen minutes of his stay. After his bill is paid, he leaves and passes two women wearing short, tight dresses and enough makeup to last for days, on their way in. Some of the men might be looking for personal entertainment tonight, and these two want to make sure they don't end up alone.

Carlos has showered and changed his clothes by the time Toño walks back into the body shop. "Ready to go?" he says.

Toño nods.

"Then let's get to it!" Carlos directs Toño to the passenger side of a pickup truck out front and both men climb inside. A ten-minute drive later, the border is in sight, a high fence with signs posted every twenty feet proclaiming the end of Mexican land. Toño thinks back to when he crossed the first time, darting between buildings as helicopters searched overhead, waiting for the window of opportunity when they could pass underneath the fence . . . it seems so long ago and couldn't be more different than tonight's relaxed drive right up to the border.

Carlos parks the car on the street. "On foot from here."

The two men walk along the sidewalk in front of a row of houses that use the border fence as a marker for the backside of their property. At the end of the row, Carlos turns north toward the fence. He walks to a spot where the fence has been cut and reattached with plastic cable ties and pulls out a set of wire cutters. After four quick clips, the ties have been severed. He picks up the pieces and puts them into his pocket. Carlos pulls back the fence and tells Toño to pass through before he closes the fence.

"You're not coming too?" Toño asks Carlos with the wire fence between them.

"No, I need to be at work tomorrow!"

Toño is stunned into silence as he watches Carlos reattach the fence with fresh cable ties.

Carlos talks while he works. "See that road over there?"

Toño turns around and sees a car drive by in the distance. "I see that car."

"Okay, that car is on the road I'm talking about." He attaches a third tie and glances at his watch. "When I tell you, run. There will be a white van that will flash its high beams twice. Get in. You have to be quick though, the van won't slow down for long because immigration would stop them."

"What if I had brought more than just my backpack?"

"Then I would have made you mail the rest of your stuff this afternoon. Consider yourself lucky."

"What about immigration?"

"What about them? If they catch you, we try again."

Toño remembers he always has a home to go back to in El Salvador, but the effect this mantra carries isn't the same as before; the years between his border crossings have diminished the ignorance that allowed him to cross the first two times without a care in the world.

Carlos finishes reattaching the fence to itself. "Good luck," he says.

"Thanks."

Minutes pass by with the two men in separate countries. Carlos stares at his watch and begins a countdown in the dark, cool night. "Three . . . two . . . one . . . Now!"

Toño runs across the space between the fence and the road as fast as his feet can carry him. He tightens the straps of his backpack to make sure it doesn't bounce on his back, then pumps his arms as he runs full speed. By the slivers of moonlight, he is able to see the rocks in his way before he clears each of them in a bound. A solitary pair of headlights approaches in the distance. He gets to the side of the road and crouches down to wait for what he hopes is the white van to get closer, the pounding of his heart deadening his senses to the rest of the world.

CHAPTER FORTY-FIVE

IN THE SAME instant that Toño can make out the shape of the vehicle, the van flashes its high beams twice and begins to slow down. Toño stands up, hoping this is the vehicle he was told to approach.

The driver of the van speeds up to close the distance between itself and the man on the side of the road. When the van is close, it flashes its lights twice for the second time.

"Toño?" a man yells out.

"Yes!" Toño replies, relieved.

"Get in!" The side door slides open and Toño comes face-to-face with a tan old man who could be Native American or Hispanic. The difference is academic; after years of mixing blood, many central Americans are both. The interior lights of the van never turn on. Toño throws himself onto the floor in the back of the van and the driver brings the vehicle back up to speed.

The driver is a white man, early thirties, with a broad, bushy mustache. There are no introductions as they drive off into the night. Each of the three men hold their breath for the next hour while they wait to see if immigration will pull them over. The driver is the first to gulp the air in the van, giving permission to his passengers to do the same.

Toño is driven halfway to San Diego before he's placed in the care of another driver, a white woman in a grey Toyota sedan. Toño tries to introduce himself, but the woman insists they not talk in case "anyone asks any questions." She talks about "ignorance" multiple times, and Toño wonders what the woman does during the day: from how clean her car is and the clean white blouse she wears, this driving can't be all she does for money. She drops Toño off at a house in the suburbs of San Diego.

"Thank you," Toño says as he gets out of the car.

The woman drives away without saying a word.

By the time Toño turns around, the front door to the house has been opened. An old Hispanic woman who looks like she could be related to his mother beckons him inside. "Quick! Before the sun comes up!" she hisses.

Toño has no idea what time it is and decides, right then and there, to get a watch and wear it at all times. He looks up at the night sky and, from the position of the moon, knows the night isn't even halfway through. "This old woman must be crazy," Toño thinks to himself.

Toño walks into the house, and the woman pokes her head outside to see if any of her neighbors have seen the arrival of her nighttime visitor. She must deem the world outside to be satisfactory, because she closes the door and turns to Toño with a smile on her face. "Do you want anything before I go to bed? Tea, a piece of cake? It's pineapple, I made it last night."

"No, thank you," Toño says. He is about to introduce himself when he decides against it, in case he's questioned.

"All right then, I'm going to bed. You guys made good time tonight!"

Toño smiles and nods.

"You can sleep on the couch. First thing in the morning we'll take care of business and get you to the airport." Toño is amazed at how well-informed the woman is. All the cogs in the gear of this operation know their roles, and he is thankful he doesn't have to worry about paying them one at a time. He wonders if Angel's crossing was this simple and makes a mental note to ask his brother the next time they see each other.

The couch is covered with fleas from cats that slink around all night, keeping Toño awake. In the morning, the old woman says it's time to settle up and Toño tries to bargain with the woman.

"Just because the crossing was easy doesn't mean it's not as valuable. Did you ever consider you might be paying for such a smooth trip? We got you here, didn't we?"

Toño studies her face, wondering how long it would take for her to resort to threats and what sort of threats she has at her disposal. Sure there are worse things these people could do than just throw him back across the border, he counts out eight thousand dollars, her asking price and a large portion of his remaining cash, and hands it over. There should be a few hundred dollars left to his name after he buys a plane ticket to D.C. She drives him to the airport before Tuesday morning's rush hour.

After Toño buys a ticket for a flight that leaves just before noon, he calls his brother.

Angel answers the early-morning phone call on the third ring. "Hello?" Angel says, his voice muffled by a thick layer of sleep.

"Angel, it's me. Can you pick me up at eight tonight?"

"You didn't give me enough time to take off work. You're lucky I'm on the lunch shift today."

"Perfect. What time is it over there?"

"Eight-thirty. I need to get up and get ready for work, I'll see you tonight." Angel hangs up the phone, and before Toño knows what's happened, he's left holding a dead receiver.

His day in the airport is spent watching his fellow travelers. The ones dressed in business attire rush to their gates, and some shuffle along the floor in sweatpants looking like they just got out of bed. Two young girls follow their parents with pillows in hand. Toño wonders about his future. How many kids will he and Lori have? What will they be like? He is excited to meet them.

His thoughts turn to darker matters. Will he be a good father? How often will he lose his temper? His stomach drops at the thought. He reminds himself about how important his father is to him and hopes that one day he has a son who understands the role discipline must play in their lives. Maybe not when he's young, but someday, he will learn to appreciate the lessons just like Toño appreciates all those his own father passed on to him.

Toño's stomach begins to rumble in the early afternoon. He holds out as long as he can against the temptation to buy food because he only wants to buy one meal, right before he boards the plane, in order to save money. When the hunger becomes unbearable, he finds a McDonald's in another terminal. He orders a Big Mac, a large order of fries, and a Coke. After the first bite, he realizes how much he missed the food on this side of the border. These first bites of food are accompanied by the feeling he has returned to America and is now in the same country as Lori, a sense that never registered during the rushed border crossing the night before.

Toño heads back to his terminal with a full stomach and dozes until his plane is ready to board. He stows his backpack in the overhead bin, rests his head against the headrest, and doesn't wake up until the pilot announces their arrival in Washington, D.C.

PART 5

MOTH TO A FLAME

CHAPTER FORTY-SIX

THE DAY after he gets back to America, Toño drives the forty-five minutes from Braddock Heights to the hotel where he used to work. The big green Oldsmobile runs like it's brand new and seems to have a mind of its own, like its destination exerts a pull that the vehicle can't resist. The dust from years of use that filled the cracks around the fixtures in the car has disappeared, and the dashboard, still cracked, shines in the sunlight.

When Toño left the hotel to return to El Salvador, he told them he would be gone for three weeks. It's been close to two months. Why did he ever tell them he would be back? The question plagues his mind the entire drive. He never had any intention of returning, but he didn't want to close the door on a job that treated him so well. Did his statement create this future for him, or was he able to predict a future that was already foretold?

Toño parks the car in his usual spot and walks through the front doors, grateful to be back. To his surprise, the hotel has undergone a transformation. New lighting brightens up the lobby, the carpet has been replaced with dark brown tile floors, and the light wood walls have either been cleaned or the new atmosphere makes them pop. Everyone seems to be smiling, at him and at each other, their white teeth reflecting light into the farthest corners of the room.

There is a line of people waiting at the front desk. Toño takes his place at the end, all the while keeping an eye out for the familiar face of an employee. The person in front of him, an older white man, turns around and remarks on the weather. He must be feeding off the brightness of the room, because he doesn't seem like the type to talk to a foreigner without reason.

"This nice in February? Makes no sense," he says, shaking his head.

After being in El Salvador and San Diego, Toño didn't notice anything special about the weather. It now hits him how odd this is since it should be cold, and he should be freezing through layers. He only has a T-shirt on and wears pants because he wears pants everywhere, no matter the climate.

"Should be a lot colder than this," he says, half to himself.

"I know! Snowed by this time last year," the old man says. He nods to the ceiling. "Bet people would use the pool if it was open."

"Next," one of the two women at the front desk says. The old man rolls his luggage forward.

William rushes towards the banquet hall on the far side of the lobby. Toño leaves the line, follows him, and before the doors to the empty hall swing shut, Toño sees his former manager with his hands on his hips surveying the empty space.

Toño takes a big breath and walks through the push doors. William turns around and almost jumps from his skin when he sees who's walked in.

"Toño!"

Toño smiles. "Hi, William."

The two men shake hands.

"You're so tan!" William says. "Did you find a new job? You

never came back."

"I just got back yesterday."

"From El Salvador?"

Toño nods.

William waits for Toño to elaborate, but Toño is busy looking around the banquet hall, happy nothing's changed inside.

"Have you come back to work or just to visit? We hired someone else for your position when you didn't come back."

"I came back to work," Toño manages to say, embarrassed.

William stares at Toño, studying his face. "We need servers for tonight," he says, searching with his words.

"My clothes are in the car."

"Go get them and help me get set up."

During the quinceañera that night, William has Toño take on a larger role than he's ever performed before. Instead of walking food out to the tables, William has Toño stand with him and direct the servers, showing him how to read the cards that dictate the meal each guest will receive. William stands with Toño in the kitchen and tells him how to determine the best time to send different waves of servers for a meal break while the chefs prepare dessert.

After the meal, William has Toño tell the servers to clear the tables, and they stand together to supervise the cleaning and putting away of all the dishes while the party in the hall gets under way.

"I think you could run this thing," William says.

Toño nods, not wanting to disagree but also not sure what kind of response the man wants.

"Would you be interested? You can't disappear again though."

"Interested in what?"

"Running the banquet hall."

"At another hotel?"

"Here."

"You run it here."

"I'm leaving, next Friday is my last day."

"So I have a job?"

"With the way you work? That was never a question. Of course you have a job! I'm offering a promotion, to be my replacement. Promise you won't skip town again and it's yours."

"I'm here to stay."

The two men discuss how much money the position pays while they put away the tables and chairs. When Toño left, he was making six per hour as a full-time employee.

"You can plan on making about eleven," William says.

They clean the floors and stand back to inspect the empty banquet hall before they turn off the lights. "Thank God you came back when you did," William says.

Even though William uses the phrase without thought, Toño does in fact thank God for the opportunity to work. After spending the rest of his money to get back to America, his situation seemed hopeless. He didn't know how he would pay rent, pay for gas, or even for food. He realizes William is a lot like the father in the parable of the prodigal son and also thanks God for placing the man in his life.

The air outside the hotel is dense with uncertainty. Warm weather in the middle of winter doesn't just confuse humans; the plants and insects also don't know what to do. After spending time with the land in El Salvador, Toño is attuned to the rhythms of the world around him and finds the silence deafening. It's like the world is waiting for a sign to blossom into spring. Even though there are still a few months left until the equinox, Toño thinks he knows what to do to wake nature from its slumber.

The car starts on the first turn of the key.

CHAPTER FORTY-SEVEN

Toño wakes up in a cold sweat the night after working late at the hotel. He knows he was dreaming, and the memory of the dream is on the tip of his tongue, but he can't seem to piece together where his subconscious took him. All he's left with is the sense he was with Lori, somewhere, either watching or communicating with her. He closes his eyes, hoping the back of his eyelids will reveal the scene to him once more, but when he wakes up the next morning he has no recollection of what transpired in his second sleep.

Today is Thursday, his first day off work and the day he has decided to find Lori. He was hoping Angel or Arminda would be able to tell him where she is, but they were both transferred to another location while Toño was away and don't know where she could be. The world still holds its breath to see if the warm weather will last, and Toño knows time is running out to bring spring into existence. If he can find Lori in time, he won't need to worry about wearing winter clothes until next year.

The search begins at the Myersville McDonald's. Toño remembers her assignment was temporary but he can't remember how long it was supposed to last. He walks into the restaurant for breakfast and is greeted by a sea of white faces all staring at the foreigner invading their corner of the world. One of the cashiers was working the last time he was here, and after waiting in line he approaches her spot on the counter.

"Is Lori here?" he asks, his heart pounding.

"Lori? She hasn't worked here in months," the young woman behind the counter says, her words enhanced by her squint.

Toño closes his eyes and exhales.

"Do you want anything?" she says, annoyed, rushing their interaction along.

Toño's hungry but not hungry enough to eat in a hostile environment. "Can I get a large Coke?"

"Anything else?"

"Just the drink."

Toño drives the forty-five minutes down to Gaithersburg with his soda in the cupholder. He can't decide whether to go to the Derwood McDonald's or Lori's house first, but either the car or his stomach makes the decision for him. He parks the car outside of where his brother and Arminda used to work. After a quick discussion with himself in the rearview mirror, he musters the courage to go inside.

"What can I get you today?" Rob, the manager who hired Angel, asks Toño.

"Remember me? You helped my brother get a job."

Rob searches his memory and after a moment is able to place Toño's face. "You dated Lori, right? How have you been?"

Toño nods. "I'm looking for her. Is she here?"

"No, she isn't. She doesn't work here anymore."

Toño feels his heart sink. "She doesn't work at McDonald's?"

"She doesn't work at this McDonald's."

"Which one does she work at?"

"Sorry, amigo, I can't tell you that. If you want to talk to her you should give her a call."

Of course Toño has already considered calling her—he doubts her number has changed—but his father always said business should be taken care of face-to-face. The more important the business, the more important it be taken care of in person.

"You want anything to eat?" Rob asks.

"I want you to tell me where Lori works."

"Listen, pal, I can't tell you that." Rob looks at the customers in line and lowers his chin. "You're putting me in a real bind here," he whispers.

"This is important."

"I'm sure it is! But there's nothing I can do for you. It's company policy."

"Then I'll go to her house."

"You do that. Now are you going to get food or not?"

Toño orders a breakfast sandwich and Rob informs him that breakfast has just ended.

"Big Mac and small fries then," Toño says, more disappointed than annoyed.

"You got it."

Toño sits in the same booth he did the first day he approached Lori. As he eats, he watches a rerun of the first time he saw her, the scene provided by the real world and the actors a figment of his imagination. Lori's walking around wiping tables and ends up at the condiment bar. In the real world, the condiment bar is filthy, with pools of ketchup and straw wrappers strewn about, but once Toño's vision of Lori passes by, the condiment bar is well-stocked and spotless, in both Toño's mind and the real world. Her specter walks back to the kitchen.

When Toño's meal is finished, he walks over to the counter

and stands at the spot Lori and he first talked. Her ghost comes out from the back and refills the straws that don't need to be refilled. Toño is about to say hello when Rob comes over, his body forcing the apparition to evaporate.

"You need to leave," Rob says. His jaw flexes as he waits for Toño to respond.

Toño, who a moment before was lost between two times, snaps back to now. He stares at the manager, and something in his eyes must make Rob second-guess his reaction because his face softens.

"Please."

Toño nods and walks out, the other customers staring.

The big green Oldsmobile takes Toño to Lori's apartment. Her car isn't outside, and Toño almost takes back control and leaves, but a nagging voice in the back of his mind reminds him she could've gotten a new car. He parks and walks up to the apartment that was almost their shared home.

The knocks on the door match his heartbeat. Three loud, deep knocks at first before his heart stops in anticipation. No answer. His heart kicks back to life and he knocks three more times, softer now, sadness tempering the nervousness. The organ recognizes Lori isn't home before Toño's aware of the fact and uncouples itself from the knocks, not placing so much stock in actions that could leave it stopped forever.

Toño walks back to his car and places his forehead on the steering wheel. The children he was supposed to have are disappearing from his future.

"What have I done?" he says to the interior of the car.

A gust of wind blows against the side of the car, and Toño doesn't need to be outside to know how cold the air is. A question from the air passes through the exterior of the car and whispers, "What can you do?"

Something has to be done for the children torn from existence before they could even be brought forth. "I could apologize," Toño says. He picks his head up when the image of whom he needs to apologize to rushes to the forefront of his mind. The big green Oldsmobile doesn't have to decide Toño's destination, because Toño already knows where to go.

CHAPTER FORTY-EIGHT

"Betty," Toño begins in a serious tone, looking at himself in the rearview mirror. He wants to get the tone just right and practices his opening word dozens of times on the twenty-minute drive to Betty's house.

The house is easy to remember because it's the last in a row of townhouses. It has a brick exterior and a barren patch of dirt below the front window where the garden will grow when spring returns. Toño parks out front and takes the steps one at a time. He knocks on the front door, ready to lay himself at the mother's mercy.

The door opens, and Betty's eyes widen when she recognizes her visitor. She lifts her chin and tilts her head as if to ask what Toño's doing at her home.

"Betty," Toño says, the same way he rehearsed. His next words, unrehearsed, catch in his throat. "I want to marry your daughter."

"Come inside," Betty says.

She tells Toño to sit on the couch, and she sits on a large pink chair off to the side. Her eyes study Toño before she opens her mouth to speak. "You obviously care about my daughter.

Why did you leave?"

"When she said she would never come back to my country I thought I was doing the right thing." He hangs his head. "I had no idea how wrong I was."

Betty nods. "You hurt Lori and now you show up telling me you want to marry her. Why should I trust you?"

Toño closes his eyes to stop the tears from falling. "You shouldn't. But if you give me a chance, I can prove to you how important she is to me. Do you know where she is?"

"No idea." After a moment of silence, she sighs and continues. "She's been staying here. Said she doesn't want to be alone in her empty apartment."

Toño sits up straight at the news. The hope in his eyes must melt Betty's apprehension, because she begins to tell him how miserable her daughter's been over the past few months. "You really did a number on her," Betty says.

A nagging concern creeps into Toño's heart that he feels the need to address. "There are a lot of people who would think I only want to marry Lori because I am illegal."

It's Betty's turn to sit up straight in her chair, in shock at the suggestion. "I've never thought that for a second!" She leans forward and forces him to raise his head and look her in the eyes. "Not one second."

"I really do love her," Toño says.

Betty nods and says, "I know."

"And I do want to become a citizen so our son can be born one hundred percent American."

The wrinkles around Betty's eyes fall towards her mouth. "If she'll take you back."

A car door slams shut out front, and both Betty and Toño stand to look through the front window. They witness Lori turn away from the big green Oldsmobile and storm up the stairs.

"Good luck," Betty says the moment before the front door flies open.

"What the hell are you doing here?" Lori screams. Her dull green skin is covered by makeup on her face, but it shows on her neck and hands.

"Honey, just listen to what he has to say," Betty says in a soft voice.

"Stay out of this, Mom," Lori says without taking her eyes off Toño. The screen door opens and shuts as the air that swirls around her escapes the house. "Well?" she says as she folds her arms.

"I came back for you."

"You should never have left!"

Toño takes a deep breath. "I'm sorry," he says.

Lori stares at Toño. When her mother suggests she listen to what Toño has to say, she tells Toño to follow her out front. "I don't want her to be a part of this."

Lori turns to Toño in front of the townhouse. "What the hell were you thinking, showing up like this?" she yells.

A gust of cold air blows from everywhere and nowhere. Lori, dressed for the warm weather, strange this time of year, shivers. "Let's talk inside your car," she says.

They stare straight ahead in the back seat of the Oldsmobile, silent. Toño is the first to turn; he tries to hold her hand. Lori pulls away. She flexes her hand, her joints stiff and her eyes still on the headrest in front of her. Toño is reminded of Jose Angel and his metal hands, the way they would be stiff in the morning. In a flash, Toño realizes Lori's made of copper, and years of neglect have left her tarnished.

When Toño's gaze returns forward, he sees her eyes staring at him in the rearview mirror. They search for something, anything, to break the anger Lori's determined to hang on to.

"Something's changed," Lori says, a cold, factual statement.

Their eyes stay glued to each other through the rearview mirror.

"You don't have the eyes of a blue dog anymore," she says.

Toño turns to Lori, and this time she turns to meet his gaze.

"It's like someone lit a fire behind your eyes," she observes.

A single flame lit inside a skull to attract a copper moth.

Lori rearranges herself, now sitting closer to Toño but not close enough for their legs to touch. "Why did you leave?" she asks.

"I don't know what I was thinking." He wants to confess his love for her, but he's afraid to be rejected.

"When you left, I thought you would turn around and come back right away. What took you so long?"

All Toño can say is, "I'm sorry," since he has no good answer to her question.

The green of Lori's skin is fading away, replaced by a reddish-brown, which has no place on her body since she hasn't been out in the sun long enough to tan.

"I'm here to stay now," Toño says. "Even after the civil war ends I'm not going back."

"You left because of the civil war?" Lori says, her words searching for a weak spot where she can attack.

"I left because you're here." The simplicity of Toño's statement quells Lori's anger before it can be actualized.

"I might be willing to visit one day," Lori says. "If we get back together, of course."

"There's some people there who will want to meet the woman I love." Toño continues when Lori doesn't respond, her mouth open in stunned silence. "You should know that I have no money," he says. He tells Lori how he spent the last of what he was able to save over the years in order to get back and promises to do what he can to create the kind of future she deserves, given the opportunity.

"If you spent the last of your money to get back, and you came back for me, you spent all of your money for the chance to get me back," Lori says.

What Toño thought might be a deal-breaker turns out to be what proves his devotion to Lori.

Lori gives in to the magnetism between them. Her leg touches Toño's, and her head rests on his shoulder. They hold hands while the greenness of her skin leaks out into the world and colors the shoots and leaves that have sprung forth from hibernation.

EPILOGUE

NATURE GIVES up on winter and allows spring to begin at the end of February. The sun shines down on the big green Oldsmobile as Toño and Lori drive to Frederick to pick up Toño's belongings. Today is the day they move him in to Lori's apartment, one of his days off. Lori, who, Toño finds out, works at the McDonald's right next to his hotel, took the day off to help.

"After we move you in, we need to take care of getting your green card," Lori says.

"Once we're married it shouldn't be a problem."

"You know how people are though, they'll think we're only getting married so you can get your citizenship. I want to get the process started."

"Maybe they're right," Toño says with a smile.

Lori hits Toño in the arm with the back of her hand. "Is that all I am to you? Your ticket to citizenship? Was this your plan all along, to get yourself an American woman?"

Toño's whole body shakes with his laughter. "You caught me!"

Lori sinks down in her seat and puts her feet on the dashboard.

"My father thinks that. He already said he won't come to the wedding."

Toño doesn't say a word. Family's a tricky subject, and he can't tell if Lori wants him to dismiss her father or commiserate with her situation.

"We'll be just fine without him!" Lori exclaims.

"Yes, we will."

Toño changes lanes. The Oldsmobile runs smoother than ever, and he's convinced it's a product of his string of correct decisions.

"Though I do think it will be a shame if he isn't around for our kids," Lori says.

"Agreed. With my parents in another country, all they'll have is your mom."

"I'm sure she wouldn't have it any other way. She's already been bugging me about invitations, the cake, the church . . . she wants us married so those grandchildren get here ASAP!"

"ASAP?" Toño says.

"As soon as possible." Lori sits up and puts her hand behind Toño's head. She stares at him while he stares at the road ahead. "I love you," she says.

"I love you too."

"Thanks for coming back."

"Thanks for taking me back."

The two of them enjoy their togetherness in silence as lane markers pass beneath them.

"Once we get pregnant we should get a two-bedroom apartment," Lori says. "There's a few available in the neighborhood, it would be an easy move."

"Another bedroom? Manuel has a baby and they do just fine in a one-bedroom apartment."

"That's different. It's expensive in New York. We can afford it."

"If that's what you want," Toño says.

"Plus, we aren't going to just have one," Lori says.

Toño doesn't have to see her face to know a smirk is pasted on Lori's lips. "How many do you want again?" he asks.

"Six."

"No way, that's way too many. Three at most."

"Three it is, then! A boy first, then a girl, then whatever God decides."

"Three boys," Toño says.

Lori turns to Toño. "No girls? What's wrong with girls?"

"Nothing's wrong, I just want all boys. You should too, it's a good thing for a woman to give her husband sons!"

"Is it now? And what should we name the first one?"

"I always thought the first one would have my name."

"Juan Antonio? No way . . ." They laugh, both knowing Lori was about to say, "Jose."

"Antonio's not a bad middle name," Lori says. "We need a different first name though."

Toño thinks for a moment. "What about Marcos?"

ALSO BY MARCOS ANTONIO HERNANDEZ

Android City Chronicles

The Return of the Operator

Before Anyone Finds Out

Good Enough in a Pinch

The Edited Genome Trilogy

Awakening

Alternative

Absolution

Hispanic American Heritage Stories

The Education of a Wetback

Where They Burn Books

They Also Burn People

Indigenous Magic

Jesus Chan and the Return of Mayan Magic

ABOUT THE AUTHOR

Marcos Antonio Hernandez writes from the suburbs of Washington, D.C. An avid reader of both fiction and non-fiction, his favorite authors are Haruki Murakami and Philip K. Dick — in that order.

Marcos graduated from the University of Maryland, College Park with a degree in chemical engineering and a minor in physics. Since graduating, he has worked as a barista, a food scientist, and a CrossFit coach.

The Education of a Wetback is Marcos's third novel.

authormarcoshernandez.com